CW01021479

Pretty Girls Playbook

GABRIELLE KERINS

This is a work of fiction. Names, characters, places, and incidents either are the product of the author's imagination or are used fictitiously. Any resemblance to actual persons, living or dead, events, or locales are entirely coincidental.

Copyright © 2023 by Gabrielle Kerins

All rights reserved. No part of this book may be reproduced or used in any manner without written permission of the copyright owner except for the use of quotations in a book review.

First paperback edition October 2023

Cover design by Kate Teves

Published by KDP
www.gabriellekerins.com

For Madeline & Lily- my forever best friends.

TABLE OF CONTENTS

1

THE MORNING AFTER

"I need a mimosa STAT," mumbled Katelyn as she shrank into the hood of her Wesleyan sweatshirt, her athletic body huddled in the corner of the greasy diner booth.

"That's disgusting. I can still taste the alcohol from last night. Honestly, the thought of drinking makes me want to projectile vomit all over this table." Tatum clutched her head in both hands.

"Hair of the dog, honey," Katelyn countered while smirking at the menu, flipping it open to the breakfast page.

"I don't need to look at the menu. I can tell the parfait will do wonders for me." Nat didn't even look up, mindlessly scrolling through her feed from the other side of the table.

"Nice one, nepomodel. Only you would crave a cup of yogurt after a night out." Katelyn was attempting to make eye contact with a waitress currently taking orders from an elderly couple. This would be the same elderly couple who'd shot judgy looks at the three girls as they'd walked in minutes before wearing stretchy black leggings and baseball hats, reeking of stale alcohol and irresponsibility.

"This woman is intentionally not looking at me," Katelyn muttered, unamused. "Like we get it. Two Early-Bird Specials. Now move on and get me my fucking coffee." Her two friends smiled and looked at each other like they always did when Katelyn was getting feisty for no reason, typically when she was hungover, PMSing, or honestly, just not in the mood.

"Ughh," Nat sighed as she threw her head onto Katelyn's shoulder. "Why do I do this *every time*," she said. "Why do we start with wine when we know that we're going to get martinis at the bar…oh my God." Her head perked up for the first time all morning. "I *definitely* gave that disgusting guy my number." All three girls snickered at the memory of the very drunk Nat, shamelessly flirting with a beady-eyed real estate analyst propped up at the bar only hours before.

"Li-ter-all-y WHY?" questioned Katelyn, still trying to get the attention of the forty-something waitress—who at this point, was definitely ignoring her.

"Wait, which one?" asked Tatum. "I feel like last night must have been a full moon or something because the creeps were *out to play*."

"When are they not, honestly," agreed Katelyn. "You know that one that I started talking to because his friend was super hot, but naturally wasn't anywhere to be found after bucktooth McGee took over the convo?" She pushed the hood of her sweatshirt to the back of her head, allowing her thick dark hair to cascade over her shoulders. "Why is it that the hot friend always disappears, and you're left with his weird college roommate who didn't brush his teeth before coming to the bar?"

"Um, I think that's a bit harsh." Tatum crinkled her petite nose when she tasted the tap water from her cloudy diner cup.

"Well, I'm glad you get a kick out of watching me dodge the Fi-Di Brads who haven't gotten laid since their sophomore year hockey formal." Katelyn arched one eyebrow. "Don't you ever get sick of pretending to be my girlfriend when we're out?"

"Never." Tatum puckered her lips and blew her friend a silent kiss from across the table.

"*Enfin,* she's coming." Nat had her eyes laser-focused on the disgruntled waitress who was making her way over in worn-down sneakers, eventually coming to a stop in front of the girls' booth.

"Listen, it's a busy morning and we're doing the best we can," the waitress grumbled with a thick Brooklyn accent, pulling out a notepad from the pocket of her apron. "So, you ready to order?"

"Um yes, we are," snapped Nat. "I'll do a Greek yogurt parfait, fruit salad on the side, and a coffee with oat milk if you've got it."

"We don't." The waitress didn't look up from her pad. "I can do half-and-half or skim."

"Black's fine," Nat conceded with a twinge of embarrassment, suddenly not in the mood to piss this woman off.

Tatum jumped right in. "Can I please get the Western omelet with a side of rye toast and a cup of English Breakfast tea?" Her voice was unusually squeaky, the way it always was when she answered the phone or ordered in restaurants. She didn't do it on purpose; she was just trying to be sweet.

"That it?" asked the waitress, glancing back at the kitchen.

"Just a mimosa, a short stack, and the turkey club for me." Katelyn folded her menu and handed it back. "And a plate of fries." She grinned at the girls. "What? They're for the table." Without a word, the woman stuck the menus under her arm and headed down the aisle.

"She's charming," mumbled Katelyn as she took her iPhone from her pocket. "And Nat, what the fuck? First of all, who orders fruit salad when they're hungover, and second of all, oat milk? At a diner? In Hell's Kitchen?" She left her questions unanswered, staring down at the stream of stories on her Instagram.

"Yeah, that was a stretch," Tatum agreed.

"I just thought I'd ask! I mean it's New York City for God's sake, and who isn't dairy-free these days anyway?" Nat retorted, fully aware that she herself had indulged in a drunk 99-cent slice on her way back uptown the night before.

"Okay wait, I want to hear all about this guy you left us to meet up with last night!" Tatum clapped her hands with excitement.

"Yeah, haven't you guys only been on like two dates?" Katelyn was still clicking through her stories, the muffled sounds of Saturday night bars coming from her phone.

"If we even want to call them *dates*." Nat rolled her eyes. "His name is John Paul. I know, not great—but he goes by JP, and he seems sophisticated. We met for *apéro* at Ampersand last week and he paid without asking me if I wanted to split it, which was groundbreaking. I mean obviously, it's still so early but we've been texting and he's going to dental school here in the City starting in the fall, so why not?" She tried to sound casual, but it was obvious she was looking for some sort of validation from either of the girls.

"Sounds *so sophisticated*," Katelyn teased.

"Ooooohhh dental school," cooed Tatum. "I want to see a picture. He sounds perfect."

"Good for you Nat, you need a little action these days," Katelyn approved. "You guys met on Bumble?"

"Hinge. Get it right."

"Whatever, if he's nice and cute—or honestly just if he's cute, I say go for it!" Katelyn did a thumbs-up. "So, give us the dirty details about last night. You guys hooked up, right?"

"Well, I didn't sleep with him," Nat blushed. "I want to try and keep him interested. I still need a plus one to Margot's wedding in September, so I'm trying to play my cards right to avoid being the pathetic Maid of Honor who can't even bring a date to her own sister's wedding." She sounded like she was trying to convince herself just as much as her friends. "But damn, I really needed some last night. I mean *you guys*—I was like gasping for it."

"Uh. We know," Tatum assured her. "But even if you just had a PG-13 sleepover, I'm sure he would still follow up for another date. I mean Nat, you're such a catch!"

"Definitely not," Katelyn corrected. "You need to *slut it up*, Nat. I mean, guys don't care if you sleep with them—they care if you *don't*. You're young and sexy, do what you want! Plus, I feel like with all this pent-up stress from work, you could use a good lay."

"A good *lay*?" Nat cringed as she leaned against the back of the divider, stretching her long legs to the opposite side of the booth. "A good lay, what are you some creepy Dad complaining to his buddies he hasn't gotten ass since his anniversary?"

"I mean let's be real, it's sluttier to blow a guy anyway, so you and Dr. Dentist should have just done the deed." Katelyn pounded her fist into her palm to illustrate, catching the attention of the elderly couple who had gotten up to leave.

"Stop it," whispered Tatum, smothering a giggle. "Granny needs a hip replacement just looking at you."

"Yeah well, Granny hasn't gotten any since before France was occupied," Katelyn said, a little too loudly.

"I guess that makes two of us," joked Nat, and all three girls burst out laughing.

"Parfait?" barked the waitress.

"That's me." Nat brushed her Chinatown Louis Vuitton wallet and dupe Celine sunglasses to the side, making room for her long-awaited breakfast plate.

"Enjoy," the waitress mumbled as she tossed the rest of the food haphazardly on the table, then quickly beat a retreat towards the kitchen.

"She's making it really hard for me to tip her," Katelyn observed, her blue eyes closing in satisfaction as she took the first sip of her murky mimosa.

"I think that man keeps staring at me." Tatum breathed out a mouth full of steam, trying not to burn herself on her hash browns. "Can I *help you, sir*?" she muttered, shooting him a glare.

"It's because you look like a hungover goddess, while the rest of us look like we just crawled out of the sewer after months of homelessness." Katelyn glanced over her shoulder, making eye contact with the gentleman sitting alone at a booth several rows behind them.

"I always wonder what goes through these guys' heads. Like does he think he has a shot? The confidence is just…" Katelyn trailed off as she shoveled a fistful of fries into her mouth.

"God Tatum, you're so lucky to have Blake." Nat nibbled at her yogurt, trying to make it last. "He's normal, he's funny, and he's *obsessed* with you. Count your lucky stars you're out of the dating game."

"Yeah, and he's *hot*," Katelyn nodded vigorously. "Speaking of Blake, his frat brother at the bar last night was *sooo* cute. What was his name again?"

"Rob," Tatum confirmed, daintily forking a bite of her omelet.

"UGH ROB," Katelyn continued. "I tried every trick in the book to get him to ask for my number, but that bitch Lauren kept swooping in. *Thirsty* much?"

"Yeah, I saw that. She was all over him—like I get it, he's a cute single guy, but everyone could tell that they weren't simpatico, and she was trying *so hard*. Never a good look." Nat held up one hand. "And Lauren's sweet. I mean, she gained a little weight after under-grad, but she's always been nice to me." She reached over the table to grab a single fry she'd been eyeing. "I think she just doesn't like you, Kate, after the whole New Year's Eve debacle."

"Oh My God, come on, that was like *over a year ago*. I mean how was *I* supposed to know they were dating? That guy came onto *me,* and I'd been drinking champagne since noon so—" Katelyn shrugged her shoulders and the other girls laughed in agreement. "Plus, she wasn't missing much *if you know what I mean*." She doused the last of her pancakes in thick, fake maple syrup.

The waitress came over and dumped the check on the table before attending to an incoming family that clearly had come from church. The three girls looked at each other and rolled their eyes. Nat grabbed her sunglasses and wallet while Tatum got up and walked to the counter, phone to her ear.

"Hi babe, I'm just paying. What's up?"

Katelyn was preparing to follow Tatum to the counter when a

man stood in front of their booth, blocking the aisle. It was the middle-aged guy Tatum had accused of staring a few minutes before.

"Hello ladies," he drawled, stroking his sunglasses. "I was sitting back there and saw you girls. I have to say, you're so beautiful."

"Aw, thank you," replied Nat with a strained smile. "That's nice of you." *Ew, did anyone ask you?* She noticed he was sporting a white T-shirt that hugged the beer belly swelling over his cargo shorts.

"You're all so beautiful," he continued lamely. "I couldn't help but notice you three sitting over here. Do you guys live around here?"

"Actually, you know what? We don't, we're just visiting. We have to go—our friend is waiting outside to pick us up. So. Do you *mind?*" Katelyn moved aggressively out of the booth, forcing the man to step aside.

"Oh, okay, that's a shame. Well, enjoy your trip," he said. He rubbed his fingers across his scruff and made his way to the door, slowing down as he approached Tatum in front of the register. In classic creep style, he gave her a head-to-toe appraisal before exiting the diner. Tatum could feel the heat of his stare and couldn't hide the red flush forming across her face. She quickly crossed her arms across her chest.

"Classic," Katelyn groaned. "*That's* the guy that approaches us. Frodo with a wandering eye." She got up from the booth and stretched.

"If I needed any more confirmation to not leave the sanctuary of my bed and Netflix for the rest of the day, that was it," Nat declared. She glanced back at the booth, making sure none of them had left anything behind. The two girls checked their phones, not looking up as they made their way to the exit where Tatum waited.

"Just Venmo me," she said. "I put it all on my card, so you can get me back in Venmo or next weekend's Uber."

"Deal," Katelyn grinned as she threw her arms around Tatum. "Want to come over and watch re-runs of 'Gossip Girl' with me?"

"You know, I wish I could, but I promised Blake I'd meet his cousin who's just moved to the City." Tatum didn't even try to mask the enthusiasm in her voice. "We're going to some afternoon comedy show on the Lower East Side," she said, shyly twirling her freshly highlighted blonde strands.

"How charitable of you," Nat declared, pushing open the glass door. "I'll come, Kate! I can't go home to the Craig's List roommate yet; she's always cooking weird shit on Sundays." She slid on her sunglasses to mask the glaring afternoon light, and the other girls followed suit. They made their way onto the busy sidewalk, alive with the ever-present shriek of sirens.

"What does everyone's week look like?" Nat asked as they idled on the street. Nobody wanted to be the first to say goodbye.

"Work, work, work, work, work," Tatum sang in her best Rihanna impersonation. "But I'll see you guys Wednesday for Happy Hour, right?"

"I've already got it penciled in," Nat said. "And if we aren't too tipsy, maybe I'll tell Dr. Dentist to come and meet us for a drink!" She lifted her eyebrows suggestively.

"He's ready to meet the family already?" Katelyn was clearly thrilled at the idea of intimidating her friend's potential new suitor. "As long as he knows he's walking into the lion's den, then tell him he might as well bring a friend for me!"

Nat rolled her eyes. "Well, if you guys don't like him then he won't last long anyway."

"If you like him, we'll like him." Tatum leaned in to give Nat a hug, signaling she would be the first to bring their ritual to an end. "What about you Katelyn, are you at the hospital this week?"

"Yup. I have clinical this week, Monday through Thursday—but trust me, Happy Hour Wednesday is the only thing that gets me through, so I'll be there." She gave Tatum a hug.

"Okay perfect," Tatum said. "Text me later. Love you guys!"

"Love you," the other girls sang out as they watched their blonde friend pull up the front of her tank top to cover her shapely chest as she made her way across the street. Her all-black athleisure outfit made her petite 110-pound frame look even smaller than it was.

"Say what you want, but I'm not giving up on my oat milk latte. Should we stop at the coffee shop on the corner?" Nat suggested, falling in step with Katelyn who was struggling to take off her sweatshirt without bumping into the other New Yorkers bustling down the sidewalk.

"You *read my mind*," Katelyn confirmed. She adjusted her barely-there white camisole, revealing an athletic midriff of olive-toned skin. "Take a right up here. We'll walk through the park to get back to my place!" She slipped her arm through Nat's, and they took off together in the afternoon sun.

2

MARCHELINE

Fifteen minutes. Nat stared at herself in the bathroom mirror, dabbing her beauty blender on the rim of her NARS foundation. She heard the apartment door slam. *Julia's home, great.* She bumped down the volume of Morgan Wallen's "7 Summers," which was softly strumming from her phone.

Julia was her roommate, the one she'd frantically sought out on Craig's List nine months before when she first moved into the City. In a fit of excitement, Nat had prematurely signed the lease on an 800-square-foot flex in Turtle Bay, planning to move in with Olivia, her roommate from Villanova. When Olivia took a last-minute job in Austin, Nat was desperate to find a roommate to split the $3500 a month rent she'd fronted when she'd signed her life (and savings) away. Even though all her friends were already locked into leases, Nat was confident she'd find a close roomie with whom she'd be just as comfortable.

Unfortunately, her visions of a shared closet and late-night

Domino's orders were soon shattered. Julia, the only "normal" respondent to her Craig's List ad, had a different ideal living situation: a distant one. The two girls were cordial, but not friends. Julia was a nurse at Sloan Kettering, and she worked four night shifts a week, inevitably landing her and Nat on opposite schedules.

Add her passion for fermenting homemade kimchi on her days off and the perpetual stench of ripening squid and anchovy sauce, and that was more than enough for Nat to want to stay away. While they occasionally made small talk about "The Bachelor" in their teeny, shared kitchen, they were far from gossiping over a glass of wine about their latest sexcapade. Nat had resented this at first, but she eventually came to terms with their relationship. But the smell? That she couldn't get over.

Nat pushed open the bathroom door. "Good morning Julia," she said, scurrying back to the oasis of her bedroom while trying not to spill her piping hot coffee.

"Heeey," Julia replied with a soft, disinterested smile before opening the freezer and whipping out a box of frozen burritos. Her lazy top knot spilled to one side, making her halo of frizz look even more unruly. Nat watched her for a moment as she shuffled around the kitchen in wrinkled scrubs, absently shoveling fistfuls of goldfish as she stuck her chicken burrito right on the base of the microwave. *No plate. Really?*

Without replying, Nat shut her bedroom door and placed her coffee on the nightstand. She slid open the door to the overstuffed closet, far from the Carrie Bradshaw-esque one she'd envisioned before embarking on her NYC journey.

Think, Nat. What says 'sophisticated' but not 'pretentious?'—'Put together' but not 'overachiever?'— 'I can afford to be trendy' without screaming 'desperate to fit in?'

She let out a barely audible sigh and rummaged through knit sweaters, worn tee shirts, a rainbow of jeans, and ironed blouses. She finally decided on a pair of fitted black Kooples dress pants and a black silky top she'd bought from Zara the week before. Nat couldn't help but feel a pang of guilt as she shimmied into the ensemble, wondering how she was going to pay off her credit card at the end of the month.

That's a problem for future me.

She swiped a pair of mid-sized gold hoops from the shell-shaped jewelry plate on the nightstand and tousled her caramel balayaged hair. After spritzing her signature Gucci Flora dupe on her neck and wrists, Nat took one final sip of the lukewarm coffee and then dabbed her favorite lip tint on her pout.

By the time Nat walked out of her room, closing the door behind her, Julia had already retreated to her side of the apartment, a light fragrance of burrito in her wake. Nat's shoulders relaxed as she moved to the shoe rack next to the welcome mat that read. "On Wednesdays We Wear Pink."

The mat was an Etsy find she'd bought for her hypothetical apartment while she was living back home and anticipating sharing with Olivia. She slid on a pair of mid-height black Stuart Weitzman booties she'd swiped from her mom's closet and grabbed the black blazer hanging on the back of the door before she stepped into the dark hallway and locked the door behind her.

■ ■ ■

"Well, well, well. Look who finally decided to show up."

Nat refrained from nervously biting her lower lip as she stepped into the showroom. Her holier-than-thou boss, Sienna, smiled faintly as she peered at Nat over the rim of her non-prescription black frames. Nat could feel the heat of her stare as Sienna took in the look Nat had so carefully curated thirty minutes before in preparation for this very moment.

Good morning to you too, Sienna.

"I'm sorry, the subway was jammed this morning," Nat spluttered, still out of breath from a running-late jog down the sidewalk. "I was on the phone with my credit card company the whole way here. I'm supposed to be interest-free on the new credit card I got but for some reason at the end of every month, I keep getting charged interest. And I had to get the cutest Louis Vuitton skirt at a sample sale last week—as if it wasn't expensive enough—and now they're charging me more interest…" Nat trailed off.

"I'm not interested in *why* you're late, to be honest," Sienna snapped. She didn't look up from the colorful spreadsheet displayed on the screen of her Mac desktop. "I *am* interested in knowing if wearing knock-off perfume ever gets old?" She let out a dry laugh. "And I see you paired that with some fast fashion today—special occasion?"

"I spilled coffee on the shirt I had on when I left the house. I stopped in Zara just now," Nat lied, aware of how pathetic the excuse sounded.

Bitch. You know what I'm interested in? How does a 35-year-old woman with Eugene Levy eyebrows get off on bullying her junior?

But instead of saying that out loud, Nat smiled brightly. "Just let me know if there's anything particular on the agenda for today! I have to finish analyzing the inventory price sheet. Then I'm going to steam some stuff in the back."

She tried desperately to recover from her boss's verbal assault as she sat down in her swivel chair. An animated screensaver of the MARCHELINE logo rolled across the desktop.

"I'll need help with the social media calendar for next month. Go through photos from the last shoot we did and send them to me. That should give us enough content."

"Yes, of course," Nat nodded, not skipping a beat.

Social media calendar. Oh joy. It's not like I have a degree in finance or anything!

"Have the material to me by noon. I need to get it over to the creative agency," Sienna said in a monotone, eyes still locked on her screen.

"Sure, I'll have it to you by then!" Nat put her black vinyl tote under her desk.

Would it literally kill you to say please, brows?

She started opening the documents on her screen, frustrated by the idea of another day of bitch work. Despite having a Bachelor of Science in Finance from Villanova, Nat had accepted the lowly intern position at Marcheline to get her foot in the door of the fashion industry. Sure, she could have gotten a better job as an analyst at an investment firm, but Nat didn't want that. She wanted the glamour and prestige of working with designers, models, and creatives; even if it came a cost—and it did.

Nat was smart. Too smart to be sitting at a desk emailing files, filling out inventory sheets, and organizing appointments, but she'd convinced herself she had to start somewhere. She also convinced herself she could do Sienna's job ten times better than she could—and planned on doing just that.

If she was going to accomplish her dream of becoming the director of an influential fashion house by the time she was 35, Nat was willing to sacrifice. Even if that meant suffering the guilt of opening new lines of credit every few months. She needed the money to help cover rent, student loan payments, weekly grocery trip to Trader Joe's, an overactive social life, and clothes she knew were meant for a different tax bracket. But she would do whatever it took.

Ping. Nat's phone lit up with an iMessage in Just Us Girls, the lively group chat she shared with Katelyn and Tatum. At the sound, Sienna shot Nat a look. *Bitch*, thought Nat, silencing her phone. Then she read the messages:

> Tate: Why the heck is the subway so slow this morning? 😶
>
> Nat: Ugh I know. Then Sienna made a snide remark when I walked in. Like I had something to do with the thousands of union workers who decided to f up the subway
>
> Katelyn: I walked. Fuck Caterpillar Brows. Shoot me if I end up as an unmarried 35-year-old power-hungry glorified sales associate who wears FAKE GLASSES

Nat smirked before locking the phone and turning her attention to the screen in front of her. Katelyn's belittling description of Sienna made her somehow seem less intimidating. Just for a moment, it leveled the playing field. Nat analyzed her agenda for the day, glancing over appointment requests and bridal inquiries before her eyes landed on INTERVIEWS 2 PM written in bold letters.

Damn. How could I forget?

Today was the day she and Sienna would be interviewing for a new intern, after months of going over countless desperate applications. Today they would hopefully find Marcheline's next low-ranker. Nat knew how these girls felt, because nine months ago, she'd been one of them. She also knew that interviewing would mean there would be two interns competing for a permanent contract in a few months, but Nat was confident she would be the priority pick. She was excited at the prospect of meeting a potential co-worker with whom she could commiserate. She also took comfort in the idea that the new girl would have to prove herself, the same way Nat had. It wasn't *exactly* a promotion, but now there would be someone even lower than her in the room, which weirdly felt like progress.

■ ■ ■

"If you're going to Starbucks on your lunch break, get me a coffee. I'm going to need it with the hellish afternoon I have." Sienna handed Nat her credit card, intentionally not giving her a choice.

"Sure, just text me what you want, and I'll be back in ten." Nat forced a smile as she took the card and shoved it in her bag.

Sienna turned back to the screen in front of her without a word of thanks, chewing her third stick of Orbit—a neurotic habit Nat attributed to suppressed ADHD. Slinging her bag on her shoulder, Nat took her time strolling through the showroom. This was her favorite part about work, when she had a minute to admire the gorgeous dresses, blouses, and coats that lined the room on glossy racks and velvet hangers.

With the simplest black silk slip dress priced at $2,400, she couldn't afford anything there, but it didn't matter. Marcheline clothes and accessories were a constant reminder of the life she craved; the life she'd been working so hard to achieve one day. She already had an internship with a top designer. She was already known among her friends as "Nat with the super-cool job at Marcheline." And she wasn't going to let her lack of money or her spiteful boss get in the way of a goal she knew she deserved. That's why she loved the showroom; it was the one thing that made everything worth it.

■ ■ ■

"So, Poppy. You've had a lot of exposure in the industry." Sienna up-and-downed the young twenty-something. "I'm curious though, what makes *you* so special? I mean, with so many people desperate for this job. Why should I pick *you*?" She sipped from her venti iced almond milk latte, a gesture Nat couldn't help but think of as unprofessional in the midst of an interview.

"Wow, I'm so glad you asked that!" The young girl crossed her legs, nervously running her fingers through freshly blown-out brown locks.

No, you're not. Everyone hates that question and you're about to bullshit an answer just like the rest of us.

Nat watched the girl intensely, noticing her every move, and channeling more of Sienna's energy than she intended.

Damn. I mean she IS chic.

Nat couldn't help but admire Poppy's fresh charcoal grey Russian gel manicure and her perfectly enhanced lips. She looked terrified, yes—but undeniably gorgeous in her oversized Dolce and Gabbana blazer, leather pants, and suede Gucci loafers. The same ones Nat had been eyeing for months but couldn't quite swing.

Family money, I bet.

Nat raised an eyebrow in an unconscious expression of jealousy.

"I don't just want to work for *any* designer; I want to work for Marcheline. I don't shy away from hard work, and I know I can be a real asset to the brand. This would be the opportunity of a lifetime." Poppy's lips twitched when she smiled, something Nat noticed because she'd been in the same hot seat herself not so long ago.

"Mmm," Sienna wiped the condensation from her cup. "As it happens, we're pressed for support. We need fewer 'thinkers' and more 'doers,' so your immediate availability may align here. We'll be in touch." She put out her hand, and Poppy got the message. Stumbling over her words, she thanked Nat and Sienna for their time and consideration, slung her Prada cross-body over her shoulder, and practically raced out of the showroom.

Nat turned to Sienna, who was scanning Poppy's resume. "I liked her," she ventured, trying to gauge her boss's impression.

"Hm," Sienna sniffed.

But Nat only cared about one question. "So, if you were to hire her, would she come to Paris?"

Sienna looked up from the resume with a smirk. "Would it be an issue if she did?" They'd been preparing for the annual pre-fall trip to Paris, and this year Nat was supposed to come along. Although they would only be in France for two days, she was beyond excited.

"No, not at all. I think it would be fun." Nat tried to sound blasé.

Of course, it's a problem if she comes. That's my trip!

"Well, I hate to burst your bubble, but no, she wouldn't." Sienna rose and walked back to her desk. "The two of us together is already plenty. I don't know if I could handle *two* interns." She sat down and began clicking at her computer.

Nat bit her tongue.

Well, I can barely handle one bitchy boss.

3

"GOD BLESS EVERETT'S IT"

"Sorry, just one second." Tatum burrowed through Nature Valley bars and crumpled receipts at the bottom of her oversized leather work bag. "I'm sure it's in here—oh, found it!" She smiled with relief as she yanked on the black lanyard attached to her Everett ID badge, slinging it over her neck.

EVERETT & BURN LTD
INVESTMENT MANAGEMENT
CYBERSECURITY AND TECHNOLOGY SPECIALIST
TATUM KELLEY

The security guard looked pointedly at her chest before landing his gaze on the card. She looked away, avoiding the discomfort of his stare. Aside from spelling out her name and title, Tatum's ID card included a photo of her perfect smile, beaming blue eyes, and tousled blonde hair. The guard leered at her picture.

"*Very* nice," he nodded.

"Thank you so much, have a great day!" Tatum mumbled,

escaping to take her place in front of the mirrored elevator bank. She felt hot under the stares of other investment bankers and analysts grouped in the lobby.

Is this outfit too revealing for work?

She was wearing a grey turtleneck and a knee-length pencil skirt with patent leather flats—but despite her conservative attire, she suddenly felt naked.

Tatum was the kind of pretty you *noticed*. It wasn't only her icy blond hair that fell in silky tresses past her shoulders. It wasn't just her crystal blue eyes that could cut into anyone's soul. It wasn't even her full, smooth lips that could be an ad for Juvéderm; it was her naïve, soft nature in spite of her looks that drew people in. More specifically, Tatum drew *men* in.

"Baywatch body with the face of an angel," is how Nat described her once. "Tits on a stick" was Katelyn's go-to compliment. But despite all the never-ending praise for her external beauty, Tatum couldn't help but feel insecure. Shrouded in self-consciousness, she felt most at home in high-neck blouses and drab, neutral colors.

"Please, after you," she heard as she looked up from her phone. The elevator opened with a *ping*, and four young finance bros watched her hesitate. One of them was a handsome, curly-headed guy about her age.

Must be a junior analyst?

"Oh, um, thank you." Tatum eased her way into the elevator, careful not to make physical contact with any of the men already inside. She stuck her hand out to push the button, preparing for a long and somewhat uncomfortable ride, when the guy put his hand over hers.

"Which floor for you?" he asked, flashing a confident grin.

"Cybersecurity floor please. It's the 58th." She glanced up. They shared a moment of intense eye contact before she tore her gaze away, feeling her face flush. The ride up was silent, first stopping on the 23rd floor, then the 36th, and what felt like a lifetime later, the 58th.

The elevator opened and Tatum stepped out. As the doors closed behind her, she heard one of the men inside mutter, "God bless Everett's IT." The others chuckled in agreement. She felt a familiar lump of embarrassment in her throat, but tucked her blonde hair behind her ears, and shook off yet another uncomfortable comment.

"Morning Thomas," she called out, approaching the front desk. She couldn't help but smile as the flamboyant redhead threw his hand up in the air and snapped.

"*Damn* girl, I just got here, and I already can't *wait* to jailbreak this bitch for lunch," he quipped as the desk phone lit up with a familiar ring.

Rolling his eyes, he picked up the phone and placed his perfectly manicured hand over the receiver. "I'll swing by your desk at 12:30. I want to try that new sushi-burrito stand today," he stage whispered, before reciting the usual sing-song greeting into the phone. "Everett's IT Cybersecurity Department, how may I help yooooou?"

"Can't wait," Tatum said as she walked past rows and rows of multi-screen desktops, routers, and widescreen trading monitors mounted on the walls. This might not be the heart of investment banking, but it's what made the industry possible, and Tatum took pride in her work.

She'd always been fascinated by computers and their endless potential, so when she'd decided on the University of Virginia, the choice to pursue a degree in Cybersecurity Management was an easy one. Despite having been one of the few girls in the predominately male classes, Tatum always felt confident in her merit and ambitions, never minding being in the minority. It wasn't until she'd started working as a CS specialist at one of the top-tier global investment banking firms that she started to feel uncomfortable, even self-conscious as a woman in her field. Not because of the competition, but because of how she was perceived—and the assumptions people made about her.

"Hey, Tatum." Her thirty-something boss, Danny, sat on a leather couch near a clear top table in an area separate from the computers. He sipped from a sloppily stained cup of coffee. He looked up, the blue glare from his computer glasses making it harder to see his kind brown eyes. Some might have found the small stain on his rumpled white polo off-putting, but Tatum couldn't help but feel charmed by his disarray.

"I wasn't sure if you'd already had coffee this morning, but Starbucks gave me extra when they messed up my order, so if you'd like, it's all yours." He gestured to the other paper cup on the glass table.

That's a lie, Tatum thought, but she picked up the cup.

"Thank you so much, Danny! I haven't had any yet, so you're *such* a lifesaver!"

Tatum had, in fact, had a substantial amount of coffee that morning, but she didn't want to make Danny feel bad for bringing her a gift. Blake had poured her a near-overflowing to-go cup while she frantically tried to get ready after their twenty-minute morning sex put her off-schedule.

Sipping her second brew of the morning, Tatum slid into work mode. "I'm just finishing the re-configuration of the firewall upgrade, so it will be ready for installation by the end of today's trading session."

Danny smiled approvingly and nodded. They both knew drinking or eating by the hardware was prohibited, but they also both knew Danny wasn't going to say anything.

Tatum made her way to the massive double monitors at her station in the middle of the room. On her desk sat a mini pink stapler, a sticky note bearing a series of numbers and letters only she could decode, a Polaroid of her and the girls from last year's Fourth of July in Cape Cod, and her favorite picture of Blake. It was taken back at her parents' house in Wexler. He was lying on her bedroom floor with her dog, Parker, looking blissfully in love at the camera.

She reached into her bag and fished around for her phone. She was still wearing her AirPods from the commute, and hastily pressed Play to resume Frank Ocean's "Lost'" before checking the messages that lit up her screen.

JUST US GIRLS
Katelyn: Get me out of here!! It's 9 AM and I already need a pitcher of margs to the face
Nat: PREACH
Nat: This DILF just came into the showroom with his wife and he keeps eye-fucking me 👀 I don't hate it

Katelyn: HAH well it IS hump day 😜 he could be your get-out-of-student-loan-free-card!!

Tatum liked Katelyn's last message and smiled to herself before clicking on the three unread messages from her boyfriend:

Blake 💜: I hope you weren't too late for work 😸
Blake 💜: I can still taste you
Blake 💜: I can't wait to get home…want to know what I'm going to do to you?

Tatum blushed at the thought of Blake. His cool-boy attitude and those piercing green eyes that lit up every time they landed on her were exactly what made her fall for him five years ago. There was something about Blake that made her lose control just enough to throw caution to the wind and channel a side of herself she worked hard not to let anybody else see.

Getting up from her desk, Tatum made her way to the women's restroom located around the far corner of the large room. She knew nobody would be in there. After all, she was one of only three women working on that floor, and the others weren't in the office yet.

Smiling as she passed Danny, Tatum glided to the bathroom door and pushed it open, revealing the sleek, all-white aesthetic of the ladies' lounge. To make sure she was alone, she took a quick glance under the six empty stalls before walking to the middle one. She closed the door, slipping off the grey turtleneck that had made her feel so modest before, revealing a lacy black bralette that accentuated her generous chest.

She swung the stall door open, making a visual barrier in case an unexpected coworker should walk in. Staring at herself in the mirror, she slightly pulled down the center of the bralette, showing even more décolleté, while she bit her full bottom lip and tilted her head to the side. She focused the camera on the mirror and quickly snapped a couple of pictures, saving them to her camera roll.

High heels clicked on the marble floor outside. Tatum rushed to shut the stall door and pulled her grey turtleneck back over her head, then flushed the toilet and walked out as her middle-aged coworker Amy shut the neighboring stall door behind her. Running the water and pretending to wash her hands, Tatum glanced down at her sultry photoshoot, deciding the second shot was her most flattering. She tapped Send before locking her phone and walking out of the restroom.

"I'll have it by three," she called to Danny as she marched back to her desk, referring to the update she'd mentioned before.

Danny looked up. "Take your time, I'm not worried." She brushed past his desk. Tatum could feel a consistent buzzing from the phone she was holding, indicating a slew of new messages from Blake. She coyly smiled, took a sip of the coffee Danny had given her, and sat back down in front of her monitors.

■ ■ ■

Thomas set down his salmon-hoisin burrito and glanced at his phone. "Nope, huh-uh, don't *tell* me they called an HR meeting at burrito hour!"

"It's okay," Tatum soothed. "Want me to hold on to it for you?"

Thomas made a face. "*What?* Girl, putting down eight inches of girth in a matter of minutes is my specialty," he said with a wink.

"This little HR stunt however is going to cost them a sleeve of protein bars. If they're cutting into my lunch break, I'm going all klepto on their shitty snacks."

Thomas adjusted his jacket, "I'll even steal one for you," he said. As he got up to make his way back to the building, he stopped to stare at his reflection in a row of mirrored windows.

Typically, Tatum and Thomas allotted the whole 45-minute lunch break to gossiping about their coworkers, but once Thomas left, Tatum had twenty minutes to herself to catch some much-needed Vitamin D. She strolled out to Central Park and sat on a park bench, sipping a skinny caramel macchiato, the July sun beating down on her face.

Tatum knew she was lucky. Most of her university classmates were working brutal nine-to-five desk jobs at mid-level communications agencies, but she loved her work in IT. That didn't change the fact that going from a life of occasional term papers and two-dollar Tuesdays at the college bar to waking up at 7 AM five times a week was a huge adjustment. Work, Blake, and the girls consumed her life, probably in that order—so she savored any moment alone, especially in the sun since she never knew when the next one would be.

Just as she'd tuned out the homeless man talking to the pigeons on the bench across from her, someone screeched, "Tatum Kelley!" The familiar shrill voice was unmistakable.

Lindsay Maddox. Kill me now.

Tatum knew Lindsay from UVA. She was one of those orientation friends she'd tried to shake six months in, an unsuccessful attempt that had landed them in the "acquaintance zone" for the next four years. Last she'd heard, Lindsay had started her own company with the help of a Squarespace template while still trying to boost her overly edited Instagram to influencer status.

"Hey, Linds." Tatum shaded her eyes, trying her best to sound excited. "I haven't seen you in forever. How are you?"

And also—Kate Hudson herself would punch you for wearing that much Fabletics.

Lindsay flipped her hair and strutted over. "Tate, it is SOOOO good to see you!" She leaned in for an airy hug. "I've been meaning to reach out, but I've just been SO super-busy lately."

Tatum flashed a bright smile, hoping it looked genuine. "I wish you had! I didn't know you were living in the City?" A subtle jab at Lindsay, who had flooded her Instagram feed with posts about her move to the Big Apple months before—several of which had been heartily ridiculed in Just Us Girls.

"Oh *really?* Yeah, I only moved here about six months ago. I needed to get out of Boston for a change." Lindsay perched her trendy square shades on top of her mousy brown bob.

Tatum racked her brain for the next conversation filler.

Literally, I have nothing else to say to you.

"You look great," she ventured.

"Aw, thank you sweetie, that's so nice." Lindsay sounded like she'd expected the compliment.

Don't patronize me, sweetie.

"Actually, I *did* recently lose like ten pounds. I started going to this new Pilates-infused spin class and the weight just *fell off!* I didn't even try." Lindsay shrugged her shoulders to seem careless.

"Well, you look phenomenal," Tatum repeated, the words tasting even more saccharine than she'd expected. She slurped down the last of her macchiato. "I hate to cut this short, but I have to run back to work! But, uh…next month I'm having a little birthday thing; you should totally stop by if you're around."

"I'd love to! That sounds fun. I'm assuming Blake will be there too? You guys are still together, right?"

Tatum smiled, remembering Lindsay's eternal crush on Blake, "Of course, he will be. He's been planning the whole thing for a while. I'll send you an invite."

"Great! I can't wait!"

Tatum adjusted her work bag over her shoulder and turned to leave the park.

"So good to see you," Lindsay's shrill voice called after her.

God, she's so annoying, why did I just invite her? Whatever—she probably won't come.

She still had seven minutes left on her lunch break, but the prospect of spending them in even more awkward chitchat with Lindsay Maddox was somehow more unbearable than getting back to her desk early. Tatum tilted her face to the sun, bracing herself for the busy Everett lobby waiting only a block away.

4

SANGRIA SEASON

"We figured we'll start with a pitcher of each." Nat tapped the grey cushion next to her as she watched Katelyn approach through the swarms of after-work professionals milling around the crowded rooftop.

"Perfect, I need it!" Katelyn plopped down on a cushion. She leaned over and grabbed a tortilla chip from the basket next to the stone molcajete filled with guacamole.

"I hope you guys don't mind," Tatum started, as she dipped a chip in some guac. "I invited Blake's cousin. Her name's Lola. She just moved to the City and she doesn't know anyone. I met her at the comedy show and she's super cool." She threw her head back to catch the over-zealous amount of guac barely hanging onto her tortilla chip.

"Such a kind soul," Nat teased, smiling at Tatum who was still struggling to fit the mess of guacamole in her mouth.

Katelyn didn't seem to be listening. "The only invite I'm

invested in is Nat's new boy-toy. So, Nat? I think I have a toothache, when will the doctor be arriving?" Katelyn leaned back to make way for the waiter, who was juggling a full pitcher of margaritas in one hand and one of red sangria in the other.

"Well, speak of the devil, he just texted me." Nat held up her phone. "He and a co-worker are almost here."

"Thank *God*. Let's hope this coworker is *hot*." Katelyn leaned over Nat's shoulder to spy on her friend's conversation.

"Hey, Lola! Over here!" Tatum jumped up to wave at a brunette in a halter sundress who had been scanning the room from the corner of the crowded deck.

"Lola, these are my friends, Katelyn, and Natalie, but everyone calls her Nat." She scooted one chair to the side to make room for their new guest.

"Hi, I'm Lola. So nice to meet you guys!" the brunette chirped, taking the seat Tatum offered.

"Pick your poison, margarita or sangria?" Katelyn asked, reaching for an empty glass.

"I'm going to go with a marg! I do love me some tequila," the girl replied confidently, crossing her smooth legs. Her sundress rode up for just a moment before she shot Tatum an embarrassed look.

"I like you already." Katelyn poured from the half-empty pitcher of green slush before handing the drink to Lola, who took it with a smile.

"*Oh My God. He's here.*" Nat was staring at her phone screen, her voice filled with anxiety. "I need to breathe! Why am I so *nervous?*" She took a long gulp from her glass, nearly draining the sangria.

"This is going to be so fun. Relax!" Tatum assured her as she turned to scan the entrance. "Is that him?" she asked, subtly pointing to two clean-cut guys in suits near the bar. One of them was blonde, cute, and outrageously tall.

"That's him." Nat made eye contact with one of the boys, lifting a hand in greeting. He nudged his friend, who picked up his Corona as they headed over.

The guy was just Nat's type—handsome, well-dressed, and European looking. He had dirty blonde hair combed back, and a clean-shaven face that made him look younger than he was. The closer he got, the more Nat could make out his towering athletic build, accentuated by his slim-fit Indochino suit. She noticed he'd also poured his beer in a glass, another small but classy gesture Nat found overwhelmingly hot.

"Hey, how are you?" he said in a low, steady voice, flashing a big, bright smile at Nat.

"*Ciao* John-Paul! Glad you guys could stop by!" Nat got up and leaned in for a slightly awkward hug, immediately regretting the *ciao* she was trying on for size. "Um, just grab any chair and pull it up." She was trying not to sound nervous, even though her anxiety was obvious to her friends.

"Hello ladies. I'm JP. Nice to meet you. This is Connor."

He squeezed the shoulder of the less cute, black-haired boy next to him. Connor gave a close-mouthed smirk and waved at the group, without much enthusiasm. JP flashed a charming smile to compensate. "Nat told me all about you, I'm excited to have made it to the meet-the-friend round."

The two boys sat down, and Katelyn wasted no time starting right in. "So, you two have met only a couple of times, right?" She knew exactly how many times Nat had met up with JP, the most recent being the weekend when Nat had drunkenly spent the night with him. JP caught Nat's eye before answering.

"Technically yes, but I feel like we know each other pretty well at this point," he said mysteriously, taking another sip from his tall beer glass.

"Must have been quite the hookup," Katelyn commented, darting her tongue around the salty rim of her glass. She looked up to catch a deadly glare from Nat, who had turned as red as the sangria. Katelyn looked back apologetically, knowing she needed to keep her mouth shut if she wanted to avoid any hurt feelings. It only took four more pitchers of booze before the group began to feel buzzed enough to feel comfortable with each other.

"So, it's Connor, right?" Katelyn zeroed in on the black-haired boy.

"Uh, yeah," he muttered, fully staring at Tatum.

"How do you and JP know each other? Are you going to be attending dental school in the fall too? I'm studying to be a PA—"

"Work, really," Connor cut Katelyn off, drinking in Tatum's curves as she set her drink down to stand up.

Katelyn had seen this movie a million times.

I can't even toy with the ugly one tonight, huh?

"Blake and some of his friends are at Ruby's Tavern if anyone wants to go with me to meet them." Tatum smoothed her pencil skirt. The mention of her boyfriend made Connor shy away, turning his attention back to his drink.

"I'm down!" Lola said, as she reached over the back of her chair to paw at her denim jacket.

"I wish, but I have to be up early for clinical tomorrow." At this point Katelyn was looking for any excuse to go home. She was sick of fighting for the attention of one more boy obsessed with Tatum.

"Actually, I'm pretty hungry," JP said, leaning in close to

Nat's ear. The two had moved to sit next to each other and Nat had decided to spend the majority of the evening driving him nuts.

First, she touched his knee, then made prolonged eye contact, and eventually started stroking his arm when she laughed at his quirky one-liners. She had him right where she wanted him, and the sexual tension was palpable. JP pulled back and looked her in the eye, making the buzzing in her head even louder.

"Would you want to go to that place near my apartment, with the truffle mac and cheese?" he asked.

"Yeah okay," she cooed, without breaking eye contact.

"Alright, so it looks like it's me and you, Lola." Tatum was relieved that Connor hadn't tried to tag along. "Text me when you get home, Kate, OK?"

"Of course! I'm going to take the subway, so it'll be quick." Katelyn was already scrolling through the Uber Eats menu she'd pulled up on her phone, looking forward to a tipsy dinner alone.

Tatum and Lola made their way to the exit, waving one final time as they approached the dark corner near the stairs. Knowing it was time to leave, Katelyn stood up. "Nice to meet you," she said stiffly, picking up the navy canvas bag that had been squished to the back of her seat for the past few hours.

"You too," Connor replied, blandly staring down at his phone. Meanwhile JP's full attention was on Nat's body as she stood up in her form-fitting mini-dress for the first time since he'd arrived.

"Do you want to come and grab something to eat with us?" Nat said, knowing that Katelyn would turn them down. It was obvious what Nat was up to, and it wasn't Uber Eats.

"No, I'm exhausted, but thank you. You guys enjoy," Katelyn

said as she leaned in to hug Nat. "And I do mean *enjooyyyy*," she whispered in Nat's ear, wrapping her arms around her.

Nat smiled. "Shut up. I'll text you later," she said, before pulling away from her friend.

"Ready?" JP stood up. His 6'4" body towered over Nat's 5'5" frame.

"Yeah, let's go!" Nat grabbed her Marc Jacobs clutch from the couch before following behind him. The two descended the stairs and stepped out onto the sidewalk, where there was a balmy nighttime breeze. JP wrapped his hands around Nat's waist. His strong fingers made their way up to the small of her back before he leaned in to press his lips against hers.

Damn, she thought as she put her hand on the back of his neck, kissing him back with urgency.

"You know what," he said between kisses. "I think we should skip right to dessert."

Nat giggled. "My place is closer," she teased, suddenly relieved that Julia was at work and forgetting all about her plan to play hard to get. "And I definitely have something sweet there." She began kissing him again while raising her arm up to signal a taxi nearby.

■ ■ ■

Blake leaned in to kiss her. "You're so hot," he whispered, loud enough for everybody else at the table to hear. Tatum touched his face and kissed back, brushing off the slight twinge of disappointment she felt over the unoriginal compliment.

"I love you," she murmured, before cozying up to his shoulder in the booth of the crowded, dimly lit bar. To any onlooker, the two were undoubtedly in love—the intimate conversation, the habitual peck every twenty minutes, and the long unsolicited gazes made it obvious. Tatum and Blake could get lost in each other's eyes—and they did, often.

Every time she caught his emerald gaze, Tatum remembered the first time she'd seen him. Towards the end of sophomore year at the University of Virginia, she and her three roommates had decided to try their luck at getting into the exclusively senior "CEOs and Corporate Hoes" party.

Even though underclassmen were strictly forbidden, Tatum and her girlfriends had used their twenty-year-old charm and sexy secretary attire to convince one of the senior baseball players to let them in. Soon her friends got lost in the crowd of sweaty frat boys and Big Booty remixes, so Tatum made her way to the kitchen in search of the keg. There she found a huddle of senior boys standing around the alcohol—and one particularly gorgeous specimen immediately caught her eye.

He was tall—around 6'2"—and he had the kind of body you could tell was the deliberate result of consistent workouts and meal prep. He was wearing a sexy suit (best party theme ever!) and his thick, brown hair was brushed back. The two made eye contact and he immediately approached, introducing himself as Blake Spencer.

Tatum had recognized the name. Everyone knew about the infamous senior baseball athlete-slash-serial player who slept with girls only to ignore them the next day. He was a "guy's guy," spending the last days of his senior year hooking up with whatever pretty face would fall for his charisma and getting drunk with his friends for Sunday night football.

She knew he had a reputation, but she didn't care. They hooked up that night. Everyone told Tatum she'd be just another booty call, that Blake Spencer was a notorious womanizer who had never dated anyone seriously in his life. Plus, what guy was looking to settle down months before graduating college? But days of hookups turned to weeks, and weeks to months.

By the time graduation rolled around, he was asking his senior Facebook group for an extra graduation ticket for his girlfriend, Tatum. After graduation, he moved back to his hometown of Morristown, New Jersey to live with his parents and commute to his NYC job to save money. FaceTime sex and spontaneous weekend visits were enough to keep the two a couple throughout the remainder of Tatum's time at UVA.

Once she graduated, she found her own apartment in the City, where Blake subsequently moved to be closer to his office, and more importantly, closer to her. So far, Tatum had been paying the whole rent so Blake could save up for his own place, and she was happy to do it. But at the same time, she found herself hoping he'd grow out of his boyishness soon. While his nonchalant attitude had been charming when she was nineteen, she was still waiting for the man she knew he could be to show up.

"Alright you two. Get a room!" One of Blake's annoying coworkers had just finished chugging his beer, hoping to seem like an alpha in front of the girls. Tatum may have loved Blake, but she hated his friends. They were immature, rude, and entitled.

Like this guy, Trevor, sitting across the table with sweat stains on his work shirt. Every other word out of his mouth was "fuck." He spent his time shamelessly ogling girls who were so far out of his league it hurt. Tatum appraised him, unable to hide her disapproving expression.

At least Blake isn't anything like those guys.

"Aw Tatum, come on! Don't hate me," Trevor protested. "I just don't need to see you two sucking face when I'm trying to enjoy my brew, that's all!"

Tatum raised her Blue Moon to her lips. "We were hardly sucking face," she corrected him.

"B. Spence, I think your chick hates me." Trevor burst out laughing, looking at the other guys for validation.

B. Spence? What is that? Why do boys always think of the most stupid nicknames?

Tatum glanced around the bar and sighed. Blake could tell she was getting restless.

"You know what? I'm starting to hate you too, Trevor," Blake said with a grin, getting to his feet. He looked at Tatum apologetically. "Babe? You ready to head out?"

"DUUDE," Trevor groaned. "We're going to get another round. Come on, let's get drunk!" he urged.

"I have a big day at work tomorrow. I should get home." Tatum didn't care if she seemed like the bitch girlfriend; she just wanted to get out of there. Blake took her hand to help her up.

"Alright, your loss, bro. The boys and I'll be here. We're going to get some *mad chicks* tonight."

Tatum ignored him, heading for the exit while Blake let out a laugh and fist bumped his friend. Blake glanced down as he jogged to catch up to her, getting there just in time to swing the heavy door open and hold it. Tatum could feel the lonely girls at the bar staring at her with envy; jealous that she was with a stunning guy opening the door for his girlfriend—instead of being subjected to the Trevors of the world. Once they were out on the sidewalk, Blake wrapped his arms around her.

"I don't know if I can wait until we're home," he said seductively, leaning in for a kiss.

He may be fratty, his friends may suck, but God, am I glad I'm not single.

5

HEART CONDITIONS

The blue-green physician's assistant scrubs accented Katelyn's turquoise eyes, making them pop even more than usual against her olive Sicilian skin. She threw her thick black hair in a high ponytail as she walked off the hospital elevator to meet the other PA students for the start of the day's clinical. Today they'd be meeting the new residents and shadowing doctors and PAs on the cardiac floor at Lennox Hill Hospital. She pumped the wall-mounted sanitizer near the entrance and rubbed it into her hands.

"Hey Rach," she said, approaching the huddled students standing by the nurses' station. "We didn't start yet, did we?" She checked her phone one last time before dropping it in her front pocket. Her classmate, clad in identical scrubs, turned around and smiled.

"Hey Kate! No, we're waiting on some medical students apparently. I guess they thought we were on pulmonology today, so they're rearranging some schedules."

"Of course, they did," Katelyn said sarcastically. A slightly overweight middle-aged man approached the group with two younger men and a young woman behind him. He was wearing a light green button-down with a red tie—a combination Katelyn immediately recognized as awful—and a lab coat with the words "Mark Danver, MD" stitched above the right chest pocket.

"Good morning, everyone. I'm so sorry for the confusion. The department mixed up the PA and medical schools' schedules. I'm Dr. Danver, chief of the cardiac department here at Lennox Hill and an adjunct professor at Pace medical college. We're sending you guys on rounds with some of the med students and the rest will be shadowing the physician's associates." He sounded annoyed.

The two men and the woman standing behind him made their way over to the group. Katelyn and Rachel exchanged a look.

Great, we have to spend the whole day with these pricks who think they're better than us because they're in medical school.

"Alright, everyone. Check the board for your patient schedules today and we'll convene in front of Room 12A to start going over charts. I'll see you all in a few minutes."

Dr. Danver looked down at the blinking beeper, clipped onto the waist of his pants.

Katelyn was flipping through her notebook, skimming her detailed notes about patient care and cardiac diseases, when she felt a light tap on her shoulder. She looked up, thinking Rachel wanted a peek at her notes.

She nearly dropped the book she was holding. There in front of her was the most gorgeous dark-haired, blue-eyed man she had ever seen. She couldn't help staring at his eyelashes, which were thick and impossibly long for a guy.

"Sorry, I don't mean to interrupt, but honestly I could use a refresher myself," he said, his voice as smooth as butter. "Care if I take a look after you?" He flashed Katelyn a beautiful smile as he pointed at her notebook.

"Oh yeah. Of course. Take it." She handed him the book. "I'm Katelyn, a PA student from the Pace program." She put out her hand.

"Peter," he said, shifting the notebook to shake her outstretched hand. "I'm one of the asshole medical students you guys are stuck with today."

Not knowing what to say, she let out a laugh that was undoubtedly too loud for the current circumstances.

"Try to keep up," she quipped, walking toward Rachel who'd been watching the whole interaction from several feet away.

"SO HOT," Katelyn mouthed to her friend as she picked up a clipboard from the nurses' station and moved closer to Rachel. "And I just *shook his hand* like I was closing a fucking business deal."

"It wasn't *that* bad," Rachel reassured her with a grin. "Really, I think you came back from it."

The two girls walked ahead to meet the attending doctor at their designated post, but not before Katelyn took one more look over her shoulder and made brief eye contact with Peter's smoldering gaze.

■ ■ ■

Katelyn and Rachel smiled broadly as they peered through the glass windows of the nursery.

"I *can't!* They are so *freaking cute*," Katelyn cooed in a baby-talk voice she hadn't even realized she could do. She stared at the swaddled infants in their incubators as the nurses took turns checking their vitals. Whenever the girls finished lunch early, or had a rare break longer than ten minutes, they'd sneak down to the Labor and Delivery floor and watch the newborns.

Working in the fast-paced, high-stress environment of the hospital was exciting, but it could also be intensely emotional. Katelyn had initially been drawn to medicine because both her parents were seasoned medical professionals.

Her mother was a child psychiatrist while her father was an oncologist back in Connecticut. Katelyn grew up in an environment focused on helping others, always impressed with her parents' commitment to caring for vulnerable people when they most needed help. Her dad's professional passion profoundly influenced Katelyn and her older brother, Carter.

While he studied to become a physical therapist, Katelyn had set her sights on becoming a Physician's Assistant. She shadowed a PA as part of a high-school program and never lost sight of her goal after that. She'd worked hard in college, put in the clinical hours, and been admitted to the Pace University program the previous winter. For the most part, Katelyn loved her studies. She spent her days helping people in need, advocating for her patients as well as playing an active role in their recovery.

But she couldn't deny the heavy burden the work sometimes exacted. Every day she was exposed to sick and dying people, often with compounding stressful situations. Whether her patients lived a long life or suffered an unexpected tragedy—death took a toll on Katelyn. That daily trauma left her numb, which was why she and Rachel loved the L&D floor. Even though they'd learned to control their emotions around sick patients, nothing put them more in touch with their feelings than looking at six-pound bundles of joy.

Rachel glanced at her phone. "Katelyn, we have to go back in like two minutes." She sighed and tore her eyes away from the tiny infant a nurse was lifting from an incubator. "Why didn't we go into Labor and Delivery? They have the *best job*." Both girls heard the newborn squealing in the nursery.

"Ugh, I know!" Katelyn said, her eyes on a chonky baby fast asleep in the corner incubator. "How can you *not* be happy the entire day when this is your life?"

She tucked her phone back in her pocket, knowing she and Rachel wouldn't be welcomed back if they were caught taking pictures of the babies. "I can't wait to have one of my own. Or maybe ten of you little squishies!"

Katelyn thought about having a family more than most of her 24-year-old peers. Since childhood, she'd dreamed of having kids of her own. In some ways, healthcare let her channel her maternal nature without contradicting the tough-as-nails persona she liked to project.

"Alright, babies! We're going to try and come back tomorrow so we can stare at you some more. Not to be creepy." Katelyn cleared her throat to slip out of her baby voice, and the two turned back to the elevators, and headed for their afternoon shift.

■ ■ ■

As the doors slid open, a high-pitched beep sounded in the hallway. "CODE RED ROOM 112. CODE RED," squawked a wall-mounted speaker.

Instantly, nurses scrambled into action. Doctors flooded the hallway, all headed to Room 112. The two girls pressed against the wall, trying to stay out of the way. Katelyn felt a knot in her stomach. Even on the happiest floor in the hospital with such precious little patients, things could go wrong—and this was proof they did.

"Come on. Let's go before we get called out for being down here." Rachel jerked Katelyn's arm, the elevator doors opened again, and this time the girls stepped inside.

"On second thought, I don't know if I could handle their job," Katelyn admitted, once the doors were shut and the sound of the alarms faded out.

"Yes, you could. You're so nurturing! And that's what makes you excellent at your job." Rachel touched Katelyn's arm reassuringly.

Katelyn smiled. She knew Rachel was right; she *was* damn good at her job.

■ ■ ■

Katelyn shut the door to her apartment and kicked off her sensible white sneakers. She leaned against the door of the minuscule studio. First, she examined the unmade Murphy bed, then the sink full of dishes. She'd told herself she'd clean those the night before. She sighed and opened the fridge. The contents included an opened bottle of cheap Pino Grigio, half of a once-frozen lasagna, and a near-empty package of rye bread.

She grabbed the wine, pulled out the cork with her teeth, and sat on the edge of the bed. After mindlessly scrolling through her Instagram feed, stalking friends of friends from her days at Wesleyan, Katelyn took a long pull from the bottle and opened her Bumble app. She quickly clicked out of the three chats she'd started the night before with different guys she'd matched with. It had been less than 24 hours, but she wasn't interested in those conversations—they were all the same. She lay back on her pillow and began swiping

Sexy hair; swipe right.
Has he literally ever seen an orthodontist; swipe left.
Picture with his mom on a dating app? Swipe left.
Looks like he has a super nice body; swipe right.
No way, this can't be him.

She zoomed in on the unforgettable angel face of Peter, the medical student she'd met earlier that day. It was a typical profile. His first picture was a shot of him looking effortlessly sexy by a campfire with some friends, the second the classic guy-holding-the-fish-he-just-caught-on-a-boat pic. Katelyn rolled her eyes. The third one got her. Some people she assumed were his parents and sister at Peter's white coat ceremony.

Katelyn waited a minute, staring at her screen, mesmerized by his crystal blue eyes. She took another long sip of her wine.

Fuck it. Swipe right.

6

SUGAR BABY

"So basically, we need a lot of help with organizing orders for Paris," Nat explained, handing a stack of color-coded folders to Poppy. "We're going to meet clients interested in the pre-Spring/Summer collection. There's a lot of busy work stuff that has to be done ahead of time. So, your timing here is perfect!"

Poppy nodded, eagerly accepting the bundle of paperwork. "Anything I can do to help!" She perched on the chair at her new intern desk next to Nat's, legs crossed in a pair of navy Saint Laurent cropped pants. Nat recognized the snakeskin Prada kitten heels from a window on Fifth.

How does she afford this stuff?

"I'm obsessed with your outfit," Nat admitted.

Poppy looked up. "Oh please, you look so chic," she protested, appraising Nat's ensemble. "Is that from the new Celine knitwear line?" She nodded at Nat's chunky sweater as she opened the top manila folder from the stack.

"Ugh, I *wish*." Nat looked down at the decently priced knock-off she'd found at Nordstrom Rack when she'd been home in Connecticut shopping with her mom. "As much as I would love to splurge, this job barely covers the bills." She opened an Internet tab to her favorite site, "Business of Fashion."

"No, I get it," Poppy went on. "I'm super lucky. I swear if I didn't have my side gig I'd be rocking H&M every day. Not that there's anything wrong with that!" She attempted to come back from her unintentional jab at Nat. She paused for a minute, hesitating. "Actually, if you're looking to make a little extra cash, I work on the side and make ten grand every couple of months! The best part is, it's totally legit. Of course, it helps cover my rent, but I always have plenty of extra to treat myself how I want." She smoothed the thigh of her $1,200 pants.

At that, Nat looked up from her screen. "Please don't suggest what I think you're going to suggest," she said, dying to know what was about to come out of her new coworker's mouth.

"Oh!" Poppy smiled. "Not that I have anything against that line of work, but that's not what I'm talking about." She leaned in closer to Nat, glancing around to make sure Sienna was nowhere in sight. Then she lowered her voice. "I donate my eggs," she hissed, without the slightest hint of amusement.

Nat was now openly staring. "You're kidding me," she replied, unsure if it was inappropriate to laugh.

Poppy propped herself back up on her chair. "Nope, every few months the agency flies me to LA where they put me out for like 30 or 45 minutes and then *voilà*, I wake up and there are ten thousand more dollars in my checking account! I figure I'm helping people who want to have a baby and I'm making bank while doing it—well, I mostly care about the money of course," she said breezily.

"Oh, wow!" Nat was shocked. "I thought that was like a myth that girls our age only threatened their moms with... No offense—" she stammered.

"None taken. My mom would definitely murder me if she found out." Poppy leaned over to rummage through her oversized Louis Vuitton tote. "Want to see a picture of my kids?" she asked cheerily as she pulled out her new iPhone from the bag.

"Um, okay?" Nat tried to sound more curious than appalled, still slightly unsure if this was all a joke.

"I have four so far, but the couple that used my eggs for their first daughter are expecting another one this fall. They live in Amsterdam and they want me to come visit after the birth," Poppy burbled as she scrolled through her camera roll, eventually turning the screen toward Nat. "Not that I consider myself their *mom* or anything—totally the opposite! I just think they're cute." There they were— two little blond toddlers with the same deep blue eyes as the fresh-faced intern sitting in front of her.

This. Is. Bizarre.

Nat let out an obligatory "Awwwww!"

How do I even react to this?

"You look so much alike," she finally forced herself to say.

"Yeah, well my genetics are at a premium because I have light blue eyes and a high IQ," Poppy recited the information like she'd heard the comment countless times before. "If you're interested, I can refer you to my agency. They evaluate you and make sure you know all about the prep and the procedure before you sign anything. Then you can finally buy yourself something worthwhile when you go to Paris with Sienna!"

Poppy smiled encouragingly before turning her attention back to her screen. "Oh, and I really think your genetics would sell at a premium too," she added, as if she were talking about a used car.

Of *course*, Nat wanted to drown herself in designer labels.

Of *course*, she'd been looking forward to her upcoming 36-hour work trip to Paris,

But at the cost of selling her eggs?!

Yeah, the last thing I need in my life is being jetted off to LA where some freak cuts me open and harnesses my unborn babies resulting in God-knows-how-many of my hell spawn running all over the world. NO THANKS.

Nat shrugged. "I have a really low pain tolerance," was the only underwhelming excuse she could think of.

"Lot of chatting going on out here."

They looked up to see Sienna striding through the showroom in her edgy all-black ensemble, an outfit that made her look more like Chris Angel than Ricardo Tisci.

What the hell is this getup?

Nat glanced over at Sienna long enough to catch a glimpse of her faux wool crew neck sweater and the black jeans that hung too low on her slim waist. Her hair was tightly twisted into a bun. Dark rimmed glasses making her face look more sullen than usual. Nat was a little shocked at the haphazard aesthetic, so atypical for her usually pristine manager.

The two girls promptly turned their attention to their computer screens, but Sienna was already looming over them. "I know it's a short trip, but Paris is a big deal. You're going to need to look the part," she snapped, peering at Nat over the rim of her black glasses. "Try something more like what Poppy's got on. Not something so cheap."

Nat refused to get flustered. "Don't worry. I've been planning my wardrobe for weeks," she countered, trying hard not to sound bitchy.

"Good." Sienna marched back to her own desk. "You're really going to need to look the part," she repeated.

Poppy began highlighting the file in front of her. "Just say the word," she whispered. "Ten thousand dollars."

■ ■ ■

Nat lay on top of her bed in an oversized Patriots sweatshirt and boxer shorts. While her typical after-work ritual included a PureBarre class, her credit card was maxed out, which meant no more expensive workout classes. She'd been lying in her ratty pajamas since she got home, staring at her ceiling fan, and thinking.

She reached over the side of her bed and picked up the MacBook Pro that was lying on the hardwood floor. She took a deep breath and opened a new private Google Chrome window. Then she started typing: HOW MUCH MONEY DO STRIPPERS MAKE? She'd taken some dance classes when she was in elementary school. Then she remembered the debilitating stage fright that had derailed her fifth-grade performance of "The Nutcracker." Even then, she'd promised herself that was the end of her performing career.

She backspaced quickly. HOW TO MAKE MONEY WITHOUT BEING A STRIPPER, *Enter.*

Sienna and Poppy were right. If she wanted to make it in the fashion industry, she had to look the part. Poppy was all of four days into her new role and was already upstaging Nat. That absolutely could not be allowed to continue. She'd spent her savings from years of tutoring jobs and the occasional birthday and Christmas present to collect a few designer pieces over time, but the small collection simply wasn't enough to keep up.

Nat scrolled the first few results that popped up at the top of the page, carefully reading the second one: SINGLE MAN SEEKING FOOT PICS $75.

Okay, honestly not bad, she thought, as she considered clicking on the link.

Then she remembered her junior year at Villanova, when she and this cute British soccer player had been casually hooking up. He'd asked to "see more of her feet" in a sexy picture she'd sent him, and her friends had all fallen apart with hysterical laughter. She giggled to herself and scrolled past.

She analyzed the other headlines—all things she'd expected. A blend of weirdly enigmatic sexual services and the occasional dark-net hacker phishing for her social with the offer "we'll pay you to clean your computer." Just as she was about to close the window and forget her money despair binge-watching "Women Incarcerated," a simple subject line caught her eye: Just Companions.

She clicked on the link. It led to a sleek landing page that read in clean, bold type: NO SEX. NO OBLIGATION. JUST COMPANIONS. She read on: BE WINED AND DINED BY THE WEALTHIEST GENTLEMEN OF NYC WHO ARE LOOKING EXCLUSIVELY FOR YOUNG, BEAUTIFUL COMPANY.

Nat's heart rate went up. She could leave the site now and re-treat to watch cons fight over toothpaste, or peek at the photo gallery before exiting the page for good. She fought her intrigue for only a second before clicking on the tab, which redirected her to an album of glossy pictures. Nat was prepared for pixelized nude shots and creepy old men, but what she saw was nothing like that. The page was filled with high-resolution stock photos of good-looking women doing seemingly normal things—eating out at fine restaurants or walking outside of what looked like a Broadway show. But the thing that really caught Nat's attention was that they were all wearing the most fabulous clothes.

Before she even knew how she got there, Nat found herself filling out the "Meet Someone" form, festooned with more pictures of "happy couples." She was sure they were models for the site, but she didn't care. She answered the basic questions:

Height: 5'5"

Eye color: Hazel

Ethnicity: White

Weight—

Oh, come on

She thought about exiting out but then Poppy's children flashed in her mind.

Might as well take a few pounds off.

She sucked in her cheeks unconsciously.

This is ridiculous.

122 pounds.

Cup Size—

Nat glanced down at her less-than-full chest.

Anyone with real taste will understand this means I can pull off a plunging neckline without looking like a super-slut.

34A.

Hobbies: PureBarre, reading, and going to the ballet.

I've literally never been to the ballet, but I'm trying to attract the right kind of person here, right?

She uploaded a picture she'd archived from the girls' trip to Mexico last spring.

Good choice.

Nat was glowing in the image, with a tan and freshly curled hair. She wore an oxblood bodycon dress that pushed her boobs all the way up; the same dress Katelyn subsequently barfed on when she drunkenly swallowed the tequila worm.

Am I really doing this right now?

Taking one final look at the profile, Nat thought about Paris, Sienna's judgmental smirk, and Poppy's egg donation. Without hesitation, she clicked "Consent & Upload."

Almost two hours went by. Nothing happened. Unsure of the next step in acquiring a sugar daddy, Nat occupied her time by rearranging her closet.

Classic, I'm literally too ugly for someone to pay for my company. Shocking.

She was in the middle of folding a hand-me-down sweater while Lizzo belted out "Juice" from her nightstand speaker when Nat heard the familiar chime of a message coming from her computer.

Shit.

She dropped the sweater, took a deep breath, and clicked on the notification. A chat window on the JUST COMPANIONS site opened:

BigBill1: Hello beautiful :)

She froze for a minute as she contemplated responding. Then she started to type.

RedDress24: Hello Bill! I'm assuming that's short for William?

Her eyes were glued to the three little dots at the bottom of the screen.

> BigBill1: Sure is! William the third actually. My son's name is William also, so an old family name I guess you could say. What's a pretty girl like you doing in the big bad city?

Jesus, he sounds like my grandpa already. I'm surprised he even knows how to use the Internet.

She took a minute and decided she'd reply half like she was in the early stages of texting a cute guy, and half like she was emailing her grandfather—a style combination she honestly never thought she'd have to deploy.

> RedDress24: Well William the Third, since you asked, I work for a pretty well-known fashion designer. But that's probably not nearly as exciting as what you do.
> BigBill1: Fashion WOW! I'm sure you look incredible in anything, and out of anything too ;)

Ew, this is definitely not grandpa.

> BigBill1: Well, now I just enjoy myself. I've been retired for some time but before that, I was involved in the telecommunications industry.

Telecommunications industry? Okay cryptic weirdo.

She stared at his name on the screen and opened a new Google tab: WILLIAM III TELECOMMUNICATIONS INDUSTRY, enter.

A web search wasn't much, but it was all she had. Unsure if her query would yield any results, Nat looked at the plethora of articles that populated the page within milliseconds. Her jaw dropped when she started to read articles about William Hayes III and his billion-dollar fortune.

Holy shit! Is this the *William Hayes?*

William Hayes was the founder of Hayes Inc., which had been the Verizon back before texting and smartphones. The Hayes family was the modern-day version of the Vanderbilts. Nat knew that because she followed 22-year-old Hannah Hayes on social media, who was always flaunting her lavish lifestyle to her five million followers.

Play dumb, Nat.

> RedDress24: I have to say, I think that may be a little before my time.
> BigBill1: That's maybe true young lady. I assume you have read and agreed to the confidentiality clause?

Please, by all means, let's get right to the romance.

> RedDress24: I'm a big girl, Bill. I know what I agreed to.
> BigBill1: Hopefully not too big :) I'm going to have my lawyer send over a Nondisclosure agreement for your signature. Nothing personal, it's standard for all my dates.

> BigBill1: Now, about that designer, who did you say
> you worked for?

Shit, an NDA? He's RICH rich.

> RedDress24: Don't you like your girls to have a
> little mystery, Bill? All I will say is that they
> are known for their stunning gowns.
> BigBill1: Well, I would love to see you in one of
> those world-famous dresses one of these days.
> I'm sure they were made to fit a perfect body
> like yours.

Okay, here we go.

> RedDress24: Well Bill, if you're lucky, you just
> might.
> BigBill1: Lucky is exactly what I plan on being ;)
> BigBill1: How old are you? I know it says 24 on your
> profile but you can never be too sure...
> RedDress24: No need to worry, all the information
> on my profile is legit. What about you, so far
> all I know is you're a bigshot in telecom. But I
> don't have anything to go off of for a visual :)
> BigBill1: Haha. I'm glad you asked. I am seventy-two
> years old, I have brown eyes, and I stand six
> feet tall.

Seventy-two?! More like six feet under.

RedDress24: Just my type ;)

Nat had to laugh at her own response.

BigBill1: So, I see you enjoy going to the ballet. I have to say, that's unusual for a young girl your age, I'm impressed. I myself am an avid supporter of the arts. And, as luck would have it, I have two tickets to Balanchine & Cunningham this Saturday evening at 8 PM. Would you care to join me?

Balancing and what?

Nat had no idea what Bill was talking about, but here it was: the defining moment.

Am I actually going to commit to this?

She heard another notification chime, this time coming from her phone, which was still sitting on top of her speaker on the nightstand. She leaned over and nonchalantly looked at the screen, glancing over two unread messages from JP before her eyes landed on a Venmo notification that made her jaw drop: "A beautiful gown for the Ballet :)"

Slowly, she looked at her new balance. It read: $5,000.

Nat started sweating, staring blankly at the notification.

FIVE THOUSAND DOLLARS!

She had chatted with this guy about nothing for all of six minutes and she was already $5,000 dollars richer. Imagine all the other payments she'd receive! She could finally get ahead on some of her rent, and still have more than enough to buy a new wardrobe worthy of Paris. Five thousand dollars was all the confirmation she needed.

Hell yeah, I'm going through with this.

Her next thought was scarier.

Wait, it's literally been six minutes. How did he get my phone number and my real name?

7

MY BEST FRIEND'S BROTHER

"You don't care if I tell JP to meet us there in a little, do you?" Nat asked, attempting to apply her nude NYX lip liner in the backseat of the bumpy Uber.

"Of course not. Have him join us." Tatum had her phone up, filming the NYC streets through her window.

"I know. But we've known Carter for so long—he's like an older brother to us! I just feel like it would be kind of weird if he saw me and JP like all over each other," Nat replied, as the car hit another pothole.

"DAMNIT," she screeched, glaring at the driver in the rear-view mirror. She closed her compact mirror and wiped the side of her mouth where her pencil had gone rogue. "Can't Eric Adams do something about these shit roads? I'm sick of it."

Tatum put her phone down. "It's totally up to you if you want to invite JP. Personally, I think it'd be fun. Plus, Blake will be there, and it would be cool if they could meet."

Nat was staring at herself in her phone. "We'll see," she said. "I just want Carter and his friends to have fun. I can always see JP another time."

The Uber pulled up to the curb outside of Katelyn's apartment building, and the driver smirked at Nat in the rearview. "Thanks," she said in a monotone, as she stepped carefully onto the sidewalk, trying not to trip in her high sandals. She slammed the door, and the car took off.

"That driver pissed me off." She swung the door open for Tatum.

"Why? Because he made you ruin your lipstick?" Tatum stepped inside and walked towards the small elevator in the foyer.

"Well, *yeah*. But also, he gave me a weird look in the mirror, like, eyes on the road, Sir!" Nat picked at a piece of lint on her tank top.

"I feel like you're kind of on edge. What's going on?" Tatum asked. Nat didn't say anything. "Oh my God. It's Carter, isn't it?"

"What? No?" Nat shook her head emphatically, stepping inside the small elevator.

"It totally IS!" Tatum screeched, squeezing herself in next to Nat. "How could I forget you guys hooked up when we went with Katelyn to visit him at Wake Forest that time?"

Nat watched the numbers light up with each floor, her face bright red.

"Okay, fine. I don't know why he makes me nervous. We literally hooked up one time and Katelyn knows so it's not a big deal, and it was so long ago but I can't help it." Nat glanced over at her friend. "Tate, I'm literally sweating."

"And rambling. Pull yourself *together!*" Tatum fanned at Nat's hot face.

The elevator door slid open, and the two girls stepped out. "He's here with friends and you're good at keeping your cool," Tatum reassured her as they walked towards Katelyn's door. Nat took a breath and ran her fingers through her hair.

"I know. He won't try anything, plus, I'm *seeing* someone now. I'm just getting in my head." Without either of the girls knocking, the door swung open, and a smiley Katelyn waved them inside.

"I could hear you chattering out here!" she said. "You guys know Carter, and these are his friends Jack and Berkley." Katelyn shut the door behind them.

"I know, Berkley, what a bullshit name," she whispered.

Nat watched as two men she didn't recognize stood up from Katelyn's bed-couch, putting their Blue Moons on her small coffee table before coming over to the girls. One of the boys introduced himself and immediately struck up a conversation with Tatum's chest, asking her boring questions about "what she does for work," while the other slunk back to the couch to nurse his beer.

"What do you guys want to drink?" Katelyn asked, grabbing two red Solo cups from the tray on the table.

"I thought I was the bartender."

Nat immediately recognized the sexy low voice as Carter's. "I'm the big brother. I bring the booze, and I make the drinks," he corrected, taking the cups from Katelyn's grip. Nat looked up and saw his turquoise eyes—the same as Katelyn's—against his tan skin, leaving her mesmerized.

Uh-oh.

"Nat," he said, looking up from the concoction in front of him. "Still a vodka soda kind of girl?" The knot in Nat's stomach tightened.

"Last time those got me in trouble," she replied, thinking back to her younger, drunker self, climbing into the twin bed in his dorm room years before.

"That's *right*," he said, flashing a charming smile. "In that case, I'll make it a double."

■ ■ ■

"Who's ready to go to?" Tatum asked, sipping the last of her rosé. "Blake's already there and he said it's pretty crowded."

"I'm ready!" Katelyn sprayed her drugstore perfume in her hair and tossed the bottle on the couch as she slid several stray beer bottles to the trash. "Are you guys good to go?"

She turned towards the three boys and Nat, who were finishing up a messy game of Flip Cup.

"The bar is legit a five-minute walk, but we should leave now if we don't want to wait in line." She grabbed her mom's hand-me-down brown leather crossbody purse from the hook by her door.

"I agree, let's go." Jack polished off the last of his beer and tossed it in the garbage bag propped up in Katelyn's kitchen. Katelyn swung open the door, motioning for the group to mobilize.

"Ah, Kate? I'm going to just put some stuff away here," Carter called. "We made a mess, and I don't want you to have to deal with it later." He started screwing stray caps onto liquor bottles.

Katelyn frowned. "Are you sure? I really don't mind doing it later when I get back."

"Yeah, it'll just be a few minutes. You guys go—I'm right behind you."

"Mom must've really given you a speech," Katelyn snorted. "Nat, *come on!*

Nat threw back the rest of her drink and got up, tossing her cup on the counter near Carter.

"See you soon," Carter said, locking eyes with Nat right before she turned to follow the group into the hallway.

"Come on you two," Tatum yelled as they waited for the elevator. "My boyyyyyyfriend said the line is getting longer!" She was clearly feeling buzzed from her single glass of wine.

Katelyn laughed. "Your boyyyfriend," she mocked as the elevator door opened.

Nat looked back towards Katelyn's apartment door. Her friends were already inside in the elevator. "Shit. I left my phone on your couch."

"I'll just text Carter to grab it." Katelyn reached in her back pocket for her phone.

"No, I should run back and get it. What if JP texts me? I'll walk over with Carter. You guys go."

"Are you sure?" Tatum looked skeptical. She knew exactly what her friend was getting into.

"Positive. I'll see you guys in a few." She turned on her heel and made her way back to Katelyn's apartment.

This isn't a good idea.

Nat stood outside the door and contemplated changing her mind for a split second before knocking. She heard Carter's footsteps coming closer.

"Hey," he said with a huge smile, opening the door wide. "Forget something?"

Nat stared at him.

"Yes, um, my phone actually." She brushed against his chest

as she moved past him and into the apartment. "On the couch, I think."

Nat could feel the heat from his body hovering over her as she pretended to look between the couch cushions.

"Nat."

She straightened and turned her body towards his.

"Carter, this isn't a good idea," she said, looking up at his piercing blue eyes.

"I think it is," he whispered as he pressed his soft lips against hers. Nat didn't even try to resist; she wrapped her arms around his neck and kissed him back intensely. Mouth still on hers, he tilted her body back, lowering them both down to the couch.

Nat's cell phone rang in her bag by the door, and she pulled away.

"Let it ring," Carter groaned, kissing her neck.

"What if it's Katelyn?"

Nat pushed Carter off her and stood up from the couch.

What if it's JP?

She adjusted the strap of her tank top that had fallen off her shoulder and scurried over to her satchel.

"Hey," she said, nervously biting her lip. "Yeah, we're just leaving. See you in five." She clicked the phone shut and stared down at it. "That was Tatum. They got a table outside." She bent down to pick up her bag.

"We don't have to go, you know." Carter was sitting up on the couch, scrubbing at his hair. "We could stay here and tell them we got lost." He smiled at Nat and nodded for her to come closer.

Damn, why does he have to be so hot?

"Carter, we have to *go*," she insisted, half hoping he would try to convince her to stay.

"Whatever you want." He stood and stretched. "Better not keep them waiting, then."

Nat watched his buff arms flexing above his head.

Screw it.

She dropped her bag by the door and strutted over to where he was standing, locking her lips on his.

"Five minutes," she said between kisses. "We're leaving here in five minutes."

"That's all we need," Carter said, running his fingers through her hair.

■ ■ ■

"Finally!" Katelyn shouted. She and the others were chatting at a large wooden table in the middle of the outdoor patio.

"Sorry, we got caught in the line." Carter strolled towards the table with Nat close behind.

"No worries. We saved you guys a seat." Blake got up and put his hand out. "How are you man?" he said to Carter, leaning in for the signature half hug, half handshake.

"Blake, long time no see, man. Hope you're treating my girl Tatum right!" Carter nodded playfully at Tatum. "You know she's like a sister to me, so if I find out differently, I'm going to have to kick your ass."

Nat came towards Tatum and poked her in the back. "I need to talk to you," she whispered. "Bathroom *now*."

"Nat, it's not a good time," Tatum hissed through a fake smile. She was focused on a figure who was approaching the table with two beers.

"Hey."

Nat immediately recognized the voice...*JP*.

"Hey, I didn't know you were coming, like, now?" She forced a smile as she took one of the cold beers from his hands.

"Yeah, I know, but you didn't answer any of my messages, so I texted Katelyn to see if you were okay and she said you guys were on your way to Ocean Bar. So, I figured I'd meet you here." He leaned over and kissed Nat on the lips.

I hope my mouth is the only thing you're tasting right now.

She wrapped her arms around his waist and smiled up at him, praying he wasn't suspicious of her slightly distant embrace.

"I know, I'm sorry. I left my phone at Katelyn's, but I'm happy you're here," she said, resting her head against his chest. She could feel Carter's glare radiating across the table.

"I was just going to ask who here still needs a drink," JP said. "Have to make a good impression on the friends, right?"

"That's a great idea!" Nat perked up. "I could use a fresh glass of champagne. Why don't I go to the bar with Katelyn and Tate and you guys stay here?" She waved at Katelyn, who was flirting with bullshit-name Berkely.

"Katelyn," she said louder, trying to get her attention. Katelyn looked up and instantly read her friend's face.

"Us girls are going to get a drink!" Katelyn sang out, grabbing Tatum's hand and standing to join Nat.

JP handed Nat his credit card, and she blew him a kiss as the three girls forced their way through the crowd of young people, eventually pushing into a small spot at the bar.

"What's happening?" Katelyn asked, trying to make eye contact with the hipster bartender, his man bun quivering under the barrage of drink orders.

"I'm freaking out," Nat hissed, twirling the credit card in her hand. "Katelyn don't kill me but…" Nat bit her lip.

"What!?"

"I didn't really go back to get my phone. I went back to see Carter. I know he's your brother but he's *so hot* and tensions were up so we had a moment of *passion*, and now I feel sick to my stomach with JP here. I'm frazzled to say the least."

Tatum threw her head back, laughing. "I KNEW IT," she howled. "You are *so* predictable!"

Katelyn took Nat's hand reassuringly. "First of all, *ew!* Can we never talk about my brother being 'hot' again?" she said jokingly. "And second of all, I know. When Carter got here, he asked about you, and I told him to behave but you guys have always had this weird thing."

Nat chuckled with relief. "So now I don't know if I should tell JP—"

Katelyn cut her off. "Are you crazy?! You guys are just starting to get to know each other! You can't tell him!" She waved her hand, still trying to get the attention of the bartender.

"It's not like you're official with JP or anything, right?' Tatum smiled sweetly at the bartender. His pierced nostrils flared in excitement when she caught his eye.

"Hi. We're going to need three lemon drops," she said, with a flirty smile.

"You're not saying anything to JP," Katelyn confirmed. "And if he asks if something is up, *deny, deny, deny.*".

"Katelyn's right. Let her take care of Carter; you just pretend like nothing happened." Tatum agreed.

"Why am I such a slut?" Nat handed the bartender JP's credit card.

"That's why we love you!" Katelyn kissed her on the cheek, then handed her the lemon drop shot. "To being a ho!" she cheered, raising her glass.

"To being a ho!" Nat repeated.

The three girls knocked their shots on the table, clinked them in the air, and slurped them back.

"Thank you, JP," Katelyn said, squeezing her eyes shut. "Let's tell them they were out of Blue Moons and head back; I think Berkley's trying to *get it!*" She winked at her friends.

To being a ho is right.

8

GOLDEN BOY

"What's going on?" Katelyn called out frantically as she sped down the long, dark hallway that led to Tatum's apartment. Nat was already standing in front of the door marked 5B.

"I have no idea. You know Sienna won't let me text at work. I just saw her messages in Just Us Girls saying she needed us and came right over."

Nat started banging on the door with the side of her fist. "Tate, it's us! Open the door." The two girls could hear muffled sobs on the other side. They exchanged a wary look that said *what are we walking into?*

When Tatum opened the door, she looked worse than either of the girls expected. Their stunning friend, who never had so much as a blonde hair out of place, stood in front of them looking like hell. Wearing an oversized UVA sweatshirt, baggy grey sweatpants of Blake's, and mismatched fleece Christmas socks, Tatum stood motionless in the doorway, her face swollen from crying, tears streaming down her cheeks.

"Oh my God." Katelyn threw her arms around Tatum. "Tate, come here." She held tight to her friend's small, shaking body.

"She looks like roadkill," Katelyn mouthed to Nat over Tatum's shoulder.

Nat suppressed a smile and gently guided the two girls into the apartment and out of the doorway. Tatum still clung to Katelyn as the three girls awkwardly shuffled inside.

"Okay. Tell us exactly what happened," Nat said, closing the door behind her.

Tatum shakily sat down on the less-than-sturdy IKEA sectional and threw her head in her hands, attempting to breathe between whimpers. "Bl-l-a-ke," she said, almost inaudibly, before bursting into another fit of hysteria. She buried her wet face on Nat's chest.

Katelyn moved a pillow to make room and took Tatum's hand as she sat down beside them. With Tatum's head resting on Nat's lap, the two girls looked at each other, knowing exactly what the other was thinking: *Oh, shit.* A few minutes that felt like hours passed; the sound of soft crying filling the room.

Finally, Nat took a deep breath and looked down at Tatum. "Okay, sweetie. Let's do some breathing; you'll feel better. Breathe in…and exhale." She released a stream of air through her mouth in a slow, deliberate rhythm.

"Now is not the time for that crap you learned from YouTube Meditation Masterclass, Nat," Katelyn announced, making her way over to the fridge.

For the first time since the girls had arrived, Tatum smiled timidly. Katelyn swung the refrigerator door open and examined its contents, clearly on a mission to find the only thing that mattered at a time like this. The plastic shelf on the door rattled as Katelyn yanked out a full bottle of twist-off rosé. She grabbed three coffee mugs from the drying rack as she slammed the refrigerator door with her foot. Katelyn attempted to pour as she walked over to Tatum who was now sitting up on the couch, her hands wrapped around her knees. Nat was propped up next to her, anticipating another bout of tears any second.

"Here, drink this and start from the beginning," Katelyn ordered, handing her a cup. "I never liked that piece of shit anyway." She gulped the cold rosé from her own mug.

Tatum breathed heavily and sipped her wine before looking at her friends. "Well, for starters, he cheated on me," she said, her voice half furious and half heartbroken. She looked at Nat and then Katelyn. Neither were able to hide their horrified expressions. Katelyn took another sip of her wine, this one much longer.

"I knew something was up; I could just feel it." Tatum gazed mournfully down at her half-empty cup. "But it gets worse. He's been acting weird towards me these past few weeks, but I never thought it would be something like *this*." Her voice quivered. "He didn't even tell me. I found the video."

"Video." Nat sounded confused. "What video?"

Tatum closed her eyes, tears falling down her cheeks. "There's a video of the cheating."

"What do you mean, a video? Did that sick fuck make a sex tape with the slore he was cheating with?!" Katelyn stood up, irate. "God, I'm going to castrate him."

Tatum swiped at her tears. "Well, sort of."

"Tate, *what* is going on? Did Blake make a sex tape with someone else or did he not?" Nat doubled down on Katelyn's suspicions.

"I think it's just easier to show you," Tatum sighed. "Kate, can you grab my phone from the TV stand?"

Katelyn grabbed Tatum's sleek, pink phone.

"You guys aren't going to believe this," Tatum said, trying not to break down again.

Nat and Katelyn's eyes were locked on the screen as Tatum typed her password and navigated through her camera roll. She eventually stopped on a grainy tan and black thumbnail.

"I found it on his computer. I was so shocked, I didn't know what else to do, so I filmed it—just in case he tried to gaslight me and tell me it never happened."

She hit play. The blurry screen focused to reveal a clear view of Blake's desktop. The image on the machine showed a seedy motel room. The girls watched as muffled, inaudible noises radiated from the phone's speakers. Blake's athletic body walked into the frame, two white towels in tow.

"The fuck," was all Katelyn could manage.

"Ugh, just wait." Tatum handed the phone to Katelyn and got up to pace around the coffee table.

Nat moved closer to Katelyn. The two of them huddled around the phone. They watched as Blake carefully laid the two towels down on the floor by the bed. The dim lighting in the room came from a beige lamp in the corner. Tacky green paisley bedding lay rumpled on the low, full-sized bed. The wood-paneled walls made the whole place look like a cheap '70s porn set.

The muffled noises stopped. There was a clear knock on the door. Blake appeared to take a deep breath before exiting the frame. Several seconds later he returned with a tall, unattractive girl in a skimpy purple bodycon that made her orangey red hair look even more lurid.

"You're kidding me. A redhead?" Katelyn said softly as she watched the scene continue. Blake awkwardly hugged the skinny girl before he started undressing, first pulling off his shirt to reveal a chiseled chest and toned arms. He then slid his slim-fit pants down to his ankles and boyishly kicked them onto the bed.

Without saying a word, the redhead shimmied off a ratty yellow thong and tossed it aside. The girls watched as Blake lay down on his back atop the towels while the redhead slunk over, eventually standing on top of him.

"No," Nat said, ignoring Tatum's soft sniffling as she nervously paced around the coffee table. The redhead abruptly hiked up her tight purple dress and squatted just above Blake's perfect chest. Almost instantly, a steady stream of urine trickled down onto Tatum's boyfriend and eventually down to the white towels he'd laid out for the occasion.

"No. Fucking. Way." Katelyn's mouth gaped open while Nat had to cover hers.

"I don't think I can watch this," Nat said, slightly turning her face from the screen but unable to stop watching the redhead crouch and bounce over Blake's delighted face.

"Okay that's enough." Nat took the phone from Katelyn's grasp and locked the screen, tossing the phone on the cushion next to her like a live grenade. Katelyn hung her head, biting her bottom lip to stop her inopportune laughter from breaking free.

"Kate, it's not funny." Tatum was biting her nails, standing with her ankles crossed.

"I know, it's fucked up," Katelyn replied with a smile she could no longer contain. Nat covered her mouth one more time to hide her smirk.

"I mean, did you know he was into golden showers?" Katelyn asked. "On the floor of stanky motel rooms?" She didn't mean to pour salt in the wound, but she couldn't help herself. Tatum looked up, her bloodshot eyes making her irises look even lighter than they were.

"Not *that* into them."

"So, you've done this before?"

"No, I have never peed on my boyfriend!" Tatum protested. "But he did ask me once. I told him I was happy with our sex life the way it was and I wasn't comfortable with stuff like that. I never thought he would, like, seek it out from some random girl off Tinder!"

"She's from Tinder?" was all Nat could say.

"What did he type in when it asked what he was looking for? Insecure redhead with a full bladder?" Katelyn was fully giggling now.

"It doesn't matter where she's from, it's proof he's foul and fucked up." Nat's atypical use of *fuck* made her comment more comical than usual. "When?" she spat, in a fury.

"Remember when he took that Miami fishing trip with his frat brothers?"

"Guess he caught more fish than we thought," cracked Katelyn, scooting in closer to her friend. Nat bit her lip trying not to laugh, nodding at Tatum to go on.

"A red *snapper*," Katelyn muttered, just loud enough for Nat to hear.

"When I asked him how the trip was, he said it was great— they caught a bunch of fish they'd never seen before." Tatum chuckled for a moment, seeing the humor in Blake's pathetic alibi for the first time. "I just can't believe he would betray me like that after five years. He was supposed to be *the one*," she groaned as her eyes welled again.

"Have you confronted him?" Nat asked.

"Not yet; I just found the video. And you know what the worst part is? All I can think of is that trip was almost six weeks ago, and he hasn't said a thing. Just carrying on like nothing ever happened. I look like a pathetic idiot!"

"You are anything but," Katelyn interjected. "She was probably some sloppy four he peeled off the ground of a dive bar. I bet he strategically fed her Bud Heavy all night and locked her out of the bathroom. It speaks to *his* character, not yours. You did absolutely nothing wrong."

"Well, obviously I wasn't giving him enough of what he wanted," Tatum said, her voice heavy with self-blame.

"And what would that be? Urine?"

"I don't know what else I could have done. I let him live with me rent-free so he wouldn't have to commute from his parent's house in Jersey. We had sex like nine times a week—"

"Nine times a *week*?! Jesus Tatum, how are you not walking side-saddle?" Katelyn widened her eyes. "And the rent-free thing is a major red flag. What a freeloader."

"Tatum, I know this is going to be hard to hear after watching that, but he did you a favor," Nat tried to reassure her. "Plus, Katelyn's right. Did he put in any effort at all? Also, going to be honest here, I had no idea that prick was riding your coattails."

"Yeah, who lives with their girlfriend and doesn't help pay rent? And then cheats?! Fucking idiot." Katelyn was doing her best to be comforting, but she couldn't fill the long pause that lingered in the air.

"Where is he now?" Nat broke the silence.

"At work?" Tatum's voice was unsteady. "I don't even want to confront him; I just want him to get his shit and get out. I never want to see him again and I hope he has herpes."

"Um, if he has herpes, that will mean *you* have herpes," Katelyn commented. Tatum was obviously too upset to consider the implications of her boyfriend having a highly communicable STD.

Tatum groaned. "Whatever. I'm going to *die alone now* anyway so it doesn't matter. I'm never going to find someone and I'm *never having sex again!*" She finished the last of her rosé and dumped the cup on the carpet.

"Not true," Katelyn cooed reassuringly. "Plus, after nine times a week your cookie could use a break." Finally, Tatum cracked a little smile. "Everything happens for a reason, Tates. Of course, it's going to take time before you feel like yourself again, but you'll get there. We always do."

Nat opened her mouth to chime in, but then thought better of it. She'd never been in a real relationship. As much as she tried to relate to her friend's heartbreak, she didn't know how that experience felt. It was one of her deepest insecurities, and while Tatum was the one who had been cheated on, Nat wanted to crawl in a hole.

Meanwhile, Katelyn was all too familiar with the gut-wrenching pain of heartbreak and infidelity. "You know what this reminds me of," she said trying to lighten the mood. "Cole."

"Okay, no offense, but Cole didn't pee on anyone. Or did he?" Nat looked at Katelyn suspiciously.

"No, but just because he didn't pee on me doesn't make him any less a loser. Remember how much of a mess I was? I was committed to that hometown fool for four years in college before he dumped me on my ass for that Twiggy drugstore blonde just after I got accepted to Pace."

Katelyn saw Tatum starting to smile and went on. "I knew as soon as he posted her 48 hours after our breakup, he'd been cheating on me for God knows how long. Tate, I'm sorry, it's the worst feeling in the world."

Her voice went from amused to sincere. She knew what it was like to be sure you had found your person only to realize they didn't feel the same way.

Unsure how to relate, Nat grabbed both Tatum and Katelyn's hands. "Well, we're here, and we're not going anywhere."

■ ■ ■

"Should I hack her email and call her out of work tomorrow?" Nat whispered, trying not to wake a sleeping Tatum. After several more bouts of tears and endless jokes about Blake's new kink, they'd finally soothed their friend to sleep. Now she lay on the couch, the faint sounds of "Freaky Friday" coming from the television.

"You wouldn't know how to do that even if you wanted to," Katelyn said. "Tate's got like fourteen levels of security on that thing. Everett probably stored that whole pee tape on their servers."

Nat pursed her lips in agreement.

"I didn't know how to tell her tonight was going to be the easiest part of this whole thing," Katelyn mused, clearing an almost empty container of orange chicken from the wooden coffee table. "Once we leave and reality sets in, the real heartache's gonna hit like a ton of bricks."

"I think it's the *not* knowing," Nat said, forking the last of the fried rice into her mouth. "I mean, you go from knowing everything about someone, being with them all the time, confiding in them—to being completely unsure of who they are and what they're becoming." Nat tried hard to make it sound like she knew what she was talking about. And in that moment, Katelyn let her.

"I hope for her sake he *doesn't* reach out. A clean break is easier to get over, and she deserves that from him, at the very least," Katelyn said, draping a blanket over Tatum. Then she glanced down at her phone. "Okay, I didn't want to bring this up earlier because obviously, it wasn't the time, but I've been talking to this unbelievably sexy med student from my clinical."

"What?" Nat exclaimed, instantly covering her mouth and hoping her loud response hadn't awakened her friend.

Katelyn looked over at Tatum, who slept undisturbed. Lowering her voice even more, she explained. "Okay, well, *talking* is a stretch. We've just been casually chatting since we matched on Bumble literally the night after we met. If that isn't a sign, then I don't know what is."

"Oh my God, that is *totally* a sign," Nat agreed. She was debating whether it was time she told Katelyn her own little secret about a boy—well, a gentleman.

"I know, right?! I mean obviously it hasn't been long, and I don't really want a relationship right now, but I'm definitely going to sleep with him," Katelyn declared, not suppressing her excitement in the slightest.

"You go, girl, I'm all for it!" Nat decided she would wait to tell her friend about her very unsexy new relationship-slash-business venture.

"What about you and JP? I haven't heard anything since you filled me in about your post-Ocean Bar rendezvous." Katelyn raised one eyebrow while flashing Nat a devilish grin; both girls deciding to skirt around the Carter incident.

"He's good!" Nat's voice went up an octave thinking about their steamy hookup. "He came over the other night. I think I'm starting to really like him." She blushed. "So, we'll see. I'm not going to get my hopes up. You know how I get…"

"He's actually quite charming," Katelyn said in her best Nat impression, "plus I wouldn't kick him out of bed." She smiled as she bent over to slide on her white clinical sneakers. "Please Nat, no self-sabotaging this time."

"Speaking of JP," Nat's phone buzzed with an incoming message that made her smile.

Thinking about you. Free for dinner tomorrow? I can make a reservation.

"Natalie, *go*," Katelyn murmured, carefully opening the apartment door. "I'll see you here tomorrow. I'm coming straight over from work."

"Don't forget the—"

"Booze. I know!" Katelyn shut the door behind her.

Nat stared at the greasy remains of their Chinese feast, taking a seat on one of the IKEA stools below Tatum's faux granite countertop. She took out her phone, ignoring the text from JP, and wrote a new message.

How did you know when you found the one?

She hit send and waited patiently for the little grey bubbles to appear. In the wake of heartbreak, hookups, and Hayes, she needed to know it was all going to be okay—not just for Tatum, but for herself. Moreover, she needed to hear it from the one person whose opinion she trusted more than anyone—whose life experience had let her figure it all out. Meanwhile, Nat didn't even know what "it" was.

9

LOLA

Tatum sat atop a studded leather stool at a high-top table inside the dimly lit cocktail bar on East 22nd Street. She gently swirled the espresso martini in front of her as she looked around hoping to see a familiar face. It had been eight days since her breakup with Blake, and that afternoon his cousin Lola had asked if she wanted to get a drink.

After debating a reschedule for 45 minutes, Tatum convinced herself she needed to get out and see people. She couldn't get over Blake in her apartment where they'd lived together and where she'd thought they were starting the rest of their lives. Everything about the apartment was a reminder of their once-happy love affair.

The modest but cozy grey sectional where they'd binged movies and made love. The kitchen where he'd cooked his famous BLTs, which Tatum pretended to like more than she did. The queen-sized bed where he had taken her to new heights, memorizing every inch of her body.

After days of being haunted by Blake everywhere she looked, Tatum had convinced herself to throw on a clean pair of jeans and a cashmere sweater and get on the subway before she could change her mind. She needed to start moving on, she told herself. That, and she wanted to see if there was any news about Blake—since Lola was his cousin.

But now that she was outside the safety of her apartment, she instantly regretted leaving. The truth was, she didn't *want* to be at the trendy Andy Warhol-themed bar waiting for Lola. She wanted to be at home, watching bad reality TV with Blake—the version of him that had made her happy only a week before.

Tatum was watching raindrops hit the tinted window by her table when she heard a low, raspy voice.

"Don't break my heart and tell me you're waiting for someone else."

Turning her head toward the smooth British accent she took in a tall, twenty-something man with big brown eyes and a million-dollar smile. He held a lowball glass of whiskey and leaned confidently on the edge of her table.

"Actually, I am, but it's not what you think," she responded coldly. Tatum wasn't in any mood to flirt.

"Let me buy you a drink. Nobody in their right mind would keep a face like that waiting," the man said easily, taking a sip of his McCallan on ice. His eyes were locked on Tatum's, completely unfazed by the coldness in her voice.

She examined his scruffy jawline.

Blake didn't have scruff.

She checked out his white dress shirt with the top two buttons undone.

Blake never wore a button down.

She noticed the crisp shirt hugging his defined arms, and her eyes caught the polished silver cufflinks; he reeked of class.

Cufflinks?! Blake would never.

By all accounts the Brit was hot, but she barely knew how to brush her hair since the breakup, let alone accept a drink from a charming stranger. Any other girl would have been thrilled to have been offered a drink by the most handsome guy in the place, but not Tatum. Just as she was about to rebuff his request, she heard a familiar voice.

"Tatum!" It was Lola.

"Looks like your luck ran out before it even started," Tatum said nonchalantly, sipping her drink.

Out of the game for five years and I still got it.

"Oh no. I'm just getting started," the sexy stranger said. "I'll be over there if you change your mind. Sorry, I didn't catch your name." He extended his arm for a handshake.

"Tatum." She shook his hand.

"Well Tatum, your next espresso martini will taste a lot better when I buy it," he announced. "Oh, I'm Leslie, by the way. It was a pleasure to meet you."

"You too," Tatum said, stifling the urge to burst out into laughter, a feeling she hadn't had in just about eight days.

LESLIE?? HIS NAME IS LESLIE?!

■ ■ ■

"I don't care how hot you are, there are two types of guys I don't fuck with: necrophiliacs and dudes named Leslie," Lola declared, taking a seat on the stool at the other side of the table. Tatum nearly spit out her drink from laughing so hard.

Maybe it was good I came out, after all.

"But I'm glad to see you're already jumping back in the dating pool so soon after everything," Lola said, pausing to read Tatum's response. Lola propped herself up on the stool, her hair arranged in a Pamela Anderson-esque updo, tendrils of shiny brown strands framing her face. Her lips were shiny with a fresh coat of gloss and stacks of different-length gold necklaces complimented the strapless black bodysuit she wore. One chain in particular plunged past her chest, disappearing into her bodysuit. Tatum briefly took in the visual of Lola's form-fitting outfit before staring down at her drink.

"Oh no, *that* guy?" Tatum shook her head decisively. "I told him to go away; he just came up to me out of the blue." She felt slightly embarrassed, as she always did when she attracted male attention.

"I mean, who could blame him?" Lola gave Tatum an up-and-down from across the table. "I was hoping I'd see you *not* looking hot for once."

Tatum knew she was trying to be nice, but all of a sudden, she desperately wanted to change the subject.

"You should try this frothy espresso martini; it is actually *so good.*" Tatum slid her cocktail across the table.

"No. You just broke up with my dickhead cousin after dating for nearly five years. We're drinking tequila...SIR?" Lola raised her hand to get the attention of one of the servers.

"Oh, I don't know if I can do tequila, I have to be at work early tomorrow and I can't show up hungover anymore this week. My boss is running out of sympathy." Tatum was trying to convince herself as much as she was trying shut down Lola's plan, but it was too late. Lola had already caught the waiter's eye and he was on his way over.

"Hi. We'll take two shots of your house tequila with extra limes, pleeeease," Lola purred to the waiter, her glittering cat-shaped eyes widening with enticement. "No. Make that four. This one needs it." She pointed at Tatum, who rolled her eyes in response, though she was resigned.

What're two shots going to do anyway?

"I don't want to know the week you two have had," the waiter joked, placing two black napkins in front of the girls. "Four tequila shots, coming right up." He turned to head back to the bar. In two minutes, he re-appeared, this time with four overflowing shots, a saltshaker, and several lime wedges. Lola took two of the glasses, placing one in front of Tatum and holding up the other.

"A toast," she announced, slowly licking the back of her hand in preparation for the salt. "To us girls!" She clinked her heavy shot glass with Tatum's.

"To us girls," Tatum repeated, as she watched Lola throw her head back from across the table. She flashed a faint smile then downed the shot, feeling the familiar burn of the cheap tequila warming her throat, then her stomach.

"Take two?" Lola asked, lifting one of the remaining shots while sliding the other over to Tatum.

"I need a second. That one didn't go down so easy," Tatum coughed, the taste of the tequila still sharp on her tongue.

"Come on. It's like a Band-Aid! Waiting will only make it worse." Lola reached for the saltshaker but took Tatum's hand instead. "Do it for me," she said in a voice that sounded—if Tatum wasn't mistaken—a little bit seductive. Tatum's gaze moved to

Lola's décolleté, still dewy from the rain, and then to her sparkling brown eyes, which looked even more intense than they had only moments before. She could feel her face flushing.

Must be the tequila.

Tatum quickly turned her attention back the shot glass, picked it up and took a deep breath. "Cheers," she said, before slinging the golden liquor to the back of her throat.

To get it over with as quickly as possible, Tatum swallowed fast, causing some of the tequila to dribble down her lips and chin.

Yeah, that one was worse.

She quickly grabbed the lime wedge from her napkin and squeezed the juice into her mouth, her whole body tingling.

"*Damn.*" Lola pounded her empty shot glass on the table as she shook her head.

Tatum waited a few seconds before she started rambling. "So, have you heard from Blake at all? Has David talked to him?" she asked, trying to sound casual. Her inhibitions were already lowered from the back-to-back tequila assault.

David was Lola's boyfriend and by proxy, a good friend of Blake's. He was tall and handsome, just like Blake. Unlike Blake, however, he was loyal to Lola, worshipping the ground she walked on. Just weeks before, Blake had told Tatum that David was planning an extravagant proposal in Italy in the spring. He intended to take Lola to a romantic beachside dinner, then lead her to a candlelit villa where he would ask her to marry him. He'd even invited both of their families to fly in and celebrate with them the following day. Blake said he and Tatum would make a vacation out of it, and of course, Lola didn't know any of what was going on.

"Listen, I know you're probably looking for some answers, and

I get it." Lola's tone was much more serious than before. "I would be too, but David hasn't told me anything. I haven't spoken to Blake myself and honestly, I don't want to. He must've really fucked up. I mean, why would you guys just end things like that?"

Tatum could feel the disappointment radiating from her face, and Lola could sense it. "But you know what?" Lola asked, her voice picking back up. "We didn't come here so you could be reminded of Blake; we came here so you could *forget* him. Now let loose and try to enjoy yourself. Excuse me!"

She called out to the waiter again. "We're going to need two more of these." She waved at the espresso martini.

"Lola, no, I can't," Tatum tried to cut her off.

"Oh *yes, you can.*"

"Only for you," Tatum said mimicking Lola's earlier remark. *Might as well enjoy myself—I'm already in this deep.*

■ ■ ■

Lola tripped and fell as she pushed open the door to her apartment. "Owwww," she slurred, dropping her keys on the tile floor. Without helping her off the ground, Tatum burst out laughing, stepping over her while making her way to Lola's pantry.

"Where are your snacks?" she demanded, opening and slamming every cabinet in the tiny kitchen.

"Ooooohh this will do!" Tatum held up a bottle of Pinot Grigio she'd found tucked under the sink. Both girls giggled as Tatum made her way to the coffee table at the center of the small living room.

Sitting on the floor next to the low table, she shook the bottle with one hand. "Welcome to Chez Lola, where the bartender sucks but the drinks are, well, free!" She opened the screw-top white wine.

"And are the bartenders easy?" Lola wanted to know, crawling on all fours over to Tatum.

"Only if your name is Leslie," Tatum giggled, pressing the bottle to her lips. Lola sat and watched as Tatum took another gulp of wine. She watched Tatum's full lips press together as she lowered the bottle. Her eyes moved down her body, taking in the perfect curves that Tatum couldn't conceal, even in an oversize cashmere sweater.

For someone who usually called it quits after a few glasses of red, Tatum was drunk. If her giddy demeanor and uncontrollable giggling didn't give it away, her rosy cheeks and glazed-over eyes definitely did.

"You're so beautiful," Lola murmured after a brief pause, reaching over to brush Tatum's blonde hair away from her face.

"Oh, um, thank you," Tatum responded, her laughter dying down. She immediately felt her stomach twist into a knot.

What the hell is this?

"No...I mean, *really* beautiful," Lola went on, this time gently brushing the hair that hung in front of Tatum's shoulder to her back, lightly stroking her collarbone.

No way, she's not coming onto me, is she?

Tatum froze. She was unsure of Lola's intentions and God forbid she call Lola out after misreading the whole situation, turning everything awkward. Or worse, going along with it only to be called out herself. After all, Lola *did* have a boyfriend.

"You're sweet," Tatum replied.

She's just drunk, that's all.

Lola leaned in closer, gently pressing her thumb on Tatum's lower lip.

Okay. Oh my God. She's definitely coming onto me.

Before she could turn away, Lola pressed her lips against Tatum's and started to kiss her, slowly at first then more aggressively. For a split-second, Tatum maneuvered her lips to fit perfectly with Lola's, feeling an unfamiliar but exhilarating rush of pleasure.

God, she's so soft.

Lola's hands gently moved up Tatum's sweater, slowly landing on her full chest with a light grip. Tatum felt another pang of arousal, grinding her hips closer to Lola's and kissing her back, this time more aggressively.

Oh my God what is happening?!

"Lola, *what are you doing?!*" Tatum jerked her head away, suddenly stone-cold sober.

"What do you mean?" Lola sounded genuinely confused by Tatum's reaction. "You just broke up with your boyfriend! I'm trying to help you get over him."

"What are you talking about?! I'm not—*gay*. And you have a boyfriend!" Tatum stood and looked around frantically for the purse she'd carelessly flung when she first got to Lola's place.

I have to get out of here.

"What are you talking about?! YOU'VE been coming onto ME all night!" Lola teetered up from her position on the floor. Her voice had gone from defensive to angry.

"Okay, in case you missed it, I already tried to ditch a LES at the bar," Tatum snapped, resorting to awkward lesbian jokes to cover up her confusion. In a haze of denial, Tatum saw her way out and took it. She spied her purse on the chair near the coffee table, grabbed it, and flounced to the door.

"I can't believe you. GET OUT," Lola yelled, her eyes filling with tears.

"You don't have to tell *me* twice," Tatum retorted, slamming the door behind her. She stood in the hallway, heart racing. A wave of defensiveness came over her.

When did I give off lesbian vibes? That girl has some serious shit she needs to work through.

Tatum's knees felt weak, her heart beating faster every second. She stood in the dimly lit hallway, trying to catch her breath.

Or do I?

10

SACRED INTERACTIONS

Humming along to the Drake track blasting through her AirPods, Katelyn couldn't help but smile as she bounced up and down on the Stairmaster. Her phone had just lit up with a new message from Peter, the med student she'd been casually chatting with since their divinely-ordained Bumble match.

Even though she'd only met him that one time at the hospital, his sweet smile was burned into Katelyn's memory—and she knew she had to have him. They'd been chatting for a few weeks, but they'd made no real strides towards seeing each other again. So, after days of small talk about classes and apartments, Katelyn decided it was time to amp things up.

The night before, she'd boldly asked Peter if he had any plans the following evening, to which he replied his typical "no." She then invited him over to "watch a movie and chill," which was code for the obvious, to which he'd replied, "I'd love to." Fast-forward twelve hours and here she was actually using her Equinox membership—the only thing her parents still paid for—for the first time since her busy clinical schedule took over her life.

Katelyn had been single since Cole, and she was nowhere near ready to jump into another relationship. Instead, she'd been having fun hooking up with different guys every weekend and teasing all the others, never caring what other people thought about her choices. Peter's face flashed in her mind, with his long, thick eyelashes and those ice blue eyes.

Oh yeah, I'm definitely having sex tonight.

She tried to hide the smile creeping across her face.

I have my whole adult life to settle down, get married, and be boring—so why would I waste my hottest years putting somebody else first?

At least that's what she told herself. But since her relationship with Cole, Katelyn had become addicted to the feeling of being wanted. Being single meant she could have any guy she desired, and for the last several weeks Peter had been her number-one choice.

Once she got home after picking up a chopped salad from Sweet Green, a strategic this-is-the-first-time-he's-going-to-see-me-naked meal, she wasted no time in preening herself for Peter.

What am I going to wear?

She quickly slid from feeling post-gym Victoria's Secret model status to "My 600-Lb Life" status in a matter of outfits. She'd already tried on several ensembles. None of them created quite the right vibe for the stay-at-home-date-slash-dick appointment. She had to look sexy but effortless. Katelyn abandoned the idea of dressing for comfort, realizing her "chill" outfit made her look like a hungover frat boy at a deli.

God, he's going to think I'm hiding a dick under this.

She stared down at her grey sweats and quickly kicked them off, immediately abandoning the "comfy chic" idea.

He's definitely sporting the same athletic shorts he's had on all day. Guys have it so easy.

She settled on her best-fitting blue jeans and her favorite cropped Rolling Stones tee shirt. She spent an hour following a "How To Get The Perfect Simple Smokey Eye" tutorial on YouTube. Then she teased her thick dark hair to get a sexy bedhead look, before spraying her neck with an edible vanilla body mist.

A knock at the door. One last look in the bathroom mirror. She was ready.

You got this. Time to get some well-deserved Peter-perfection D.

"Hey," she said, opening the door. The confident attitude took Peter by surprise.

"Hey, how are ya? Good to see you." He leaned in for the hug. His warm, musky cologne filled the air around her.

Fuck, and he smells good.

She felt petite as she pressed herself against him.

Fuck. Me. Now.

Two bottles of wine and a few episodes of "The Office" later, and Katelyn's carefully strategized outfit was strewn on the floor, her hair a tangled mess from the consistent friction of her pillow.

"Damn," she said, rolling over to grab the day-old glass of water from her nightstand.

That was even better than I thought it would be.

Katelyn was no stranger to sex. Lately, it was pretty much all she'd been doing outside of clinical, usually by accident after a few drinks on a Bumble date. She'd never had those deliciously slutty college years like all of her friends because she'd always been loyal to

Cole. So, when she moved to the city for PA school, she embraced a much more liberated outlook.

That didn't mean, however, that Katelyn always felt satisfied after being with guys. She usually didn't. It seemed her needs were never the priority. In an age of app hookups, dick pics, and "guys who watch too much porn and fuck like jackrabbits," as Katelyn recently put it, she was used to feeling unsatisfied.

That wasn't the case now, after doing it with Peter. She still felt weak when she put down the glass of water. This time, her needs most definitely *had* been the priority. Katelyn looked over at the young med student lying next to her, his brown hair now wispily tousled across his forehead.

"There's a really bad pizza place on the corner of the block," Katelyn said casually. "I don't know about you, but I definitely worked up an appetite." She lay back down on her pillow. Peter opened his eyes and kissed her.

Fuck me again.

"I'd love to, but I have a huge Endocrinology test this week and I already took an extended study break." He nibbled at Katelyn's neck.

"Well, I'd hate to be the one responsible if you didn't pass with flying colors," she said. She was semi-disappointed he hadn't made more of an effort to stay, but she also wasn't surprised.

Peter kissed her one last time and got up from the futon, pulling up the black joggers he'd shown up in several hours earlier. She watched him throw on his white tee shirt. She felt another twinge of arousal when he stretched the shirt over his head and his defined chest flexed. Without saying anything else, he headed for the door, stopping only to slide on his sneakers.

"You were amazing," he called over his shoulder as he opened the door to let himself out. "We need to do this again." His voice faded out as the door swung shut. And just like that, silence filled the apartment.

For a moment Katelyn sat in bed, thinking about Peter, and how he'd leveled up to all of her sexual expectations.

Not only leveled up to but blew out of the water!

She opened her phone to Just Us Girls:

Katelyn: You guys…I think I'm in love
Tatum: What?! Peter?? Did he come over
Nat: OMG details!!
Katelyn: I can't even… let's just say it was life-changing and our wedding will be in approximately two years
Nat: Ok great I'll add it to my Google calendar

Smiling at her friends' comments, Katelyn got up and walked to the bathroom, where she turned the shower to the hottest it could go. Scrolling through her "Bubbles" playlist, she was still reeling from the evening when Peter's name flashed on her phone.

best study break ever

She smiled and texted back.

Glad I could relieve some of that stress.

She hit Send and flipped the phone over, nervous at the prospect of a response. Then Miguel's "Sure Thing" rolled out of her playlist just as she was hopping in the shower. Katelyn let out a girly screech. *Another sign!*

■ ■ ■

Katelyn snoozed her alarm one too many times before realizing how disastrously late she was. When she had to forego her usual coffee stop to get to the hospital on time, she knew her morning was only going to get worse. Thanks to countless hours at the hospital, keeping up with classes, and alternating "breakup support" sleepovers at Tatum's, she could barely get out of bed.

Which wasn't good. Even if Katelyn was fatigued and overworked, today was a big day. She was going to be evaluated on her cardiac clinical skills, the culmination of several weeks of forced memorization and clinical practice. She had to be on her game, but something still felt off.

Katelyn couldn't help but be distracted, thinking about Peter and the fact that she hadn't heard from him since that night at her apartment—three weeks ago. She usually couldn't care less about being ghosted. After all, she was a serial ghoster herself. Maybe it was because she hadn't received a follow-up text from him when she thought she would. Maybe it was that crazy idea she'd had that the stars had finally aligned in her favor. But with only thirty minutes to go before the exam, Katelyn had to force her thoughts away from not-so-perfect Peter to go over the last of her illegible notes.

The most common symptoms of cardiac arrest are weakness, shortness of breath, fainting, chest pain and—

Katelyn stopped in her tracks. Walking across the atrium of the hospital, she looked up and saw Peter's unmistakably beautiful profile. There he stood, sporting the same white coat she'd loved when she stalked his Bumble profile.

He was listening intently as the attending next to him spoke to a group of students. She had a brief flashback of Peter at her place. His strong arms hoisting her onto her futon. His warm tongue making its way down her body. That first thrust. Katelyn wanted to jump on him right there in the middle of the hospital.

She considered her options. She could put her head down and take a sharp right to the staircase, where she could surely avoid a potential encounter. Or she could look up casually and throw him a dazzling smile without a care in the world.

Okay, enough. I am a confident woman; I got this.

Katelyn took a deep breath and looked up, making intense eye contact with Peter for a split second before he looked away. Then the doctor finished his talk, and Peter turned away with the rest of his peers, dispersing in the opposite direction.

Did he just ignore me? Fuck!

Ducking into the staircase she'd reserved for Option A, Katelyn stood still.

Maybe he didn't see me. No, he saw me. What the hell, why would he not say hi?

She looked down at her watch, realizing she was seriously running late at this point. As Katelyn hurtled up the stairs, it occurred to her that she'd left out a critical cardiac symptom before, one that she was only now remembering—because it was happening to her.

Heart palpations.

■ ■ ■

"AND THEN he just stared at me! Actually, no he didn't even stare at me; he glanced over at me before he walked in the other direction. It was such a 'fuck you.'"

Katelyn smeared a slab of butter onto the Italian ciabatta the waiter had put in front of the girls. Nat eyed the bread without reaching for it.

"Maybe he didn't see you?" she offered, trying to get her mind off the pile of carbs that she desperately wanted to stuff into her face.

"That's what I thought at first, but he *had* to have seen me," Katelyn replied, going in for another slice. "I mean okay, he didn't want anything else from me. I get it—but that's just plain rude. I wasn't asking him to get down on one knee. A slight *wave* would have sufficed."

"Forget him, Kate," Tatum patted her arm. "You said yourself you only wanted a hookup. Yes, it was rude of him to ignore you—but forget it happened and move on. Be glad he didn't ask you to pee on him. He's a loser. How was your test today?"

Katelyn was getting upset. She looked up from the bread crust in her hands, eyes filling up with tears.

"Are you *crying?*" Nat blurted out, clearly surprised at Katelyn's reaction.

"I mean he could have at least said *hi,*" she countered, her voice quivering. She quickly wiped the tears from her face. "This is stupid. I don't know why I'm crying."

Tatum rubbed Katelyn's shoulder. "No, it's okay. Sometimes things just hit you harder than you expect them to." In truth, both Tatum and Nat were perplexed to see Katelyn break down over something she would typically classify as trivial.

She hadn't cried in Tatum's basement the night before the girls left for separate colleges.

She hadn't cried when her beloved Labrador, Dolly, died.

She hadn't even cried in front of the girls when Cole broke her heart and took up with Walmart Twiggy three days later.

She was the one who always said, "Everything happens for a reason." Until now that seemed to keep her cool and collected.

"Let it out honey, there's no place quite as cathartic as a Carrabba's Grill," Nat urged, shoving the last piece of bread in her mouth. She'd succumbed; her ciabatta craving could not be denied.

Katelyn laughed. "When's the food coming? I'm starving!" Clearly, she wanted to move on from the topic of Peter's snub. She looked over her shoulder for the waiter, hoping the girls wouldn't catch the last solitary tear that ran down her cheek.

11

BILLS, BILLS, BILL

"Okay, so do you want chicken or sofritas?" Katelyn asked, staring down at the To-Go Chipotle order page she'd pulled up on her phone.

"Both," Tatum said, curling her hair with a cheap Conair wand while sitting cross-legged on her bedroom floor. "And extra cheese and guacamole."

"I see we're watching our figure these days," Katelyn cracked, marking the order down. "What about you Nat, something nasty and healthy I'm guessing?"

"Not today. Sienna kept me on the phone all morning setting more appointments and I'm starving. I'll do a salad with pinto beans, double chicken, spicy salsa, guac, and chips on the side." Nat was flopped across Tatum's bed in a T-shirt, scrolling through her phone.

"*That's* what I like to see." Katelyn grinned as she perused the menu for more options before finally tapping in her own order. Nat watched her rummage through her wallet to find another credit card. "It's asking me to update my payment. *Classic.*" She squinted at two of her cards.

"Here. Use mine." Nat said. "My treat tonight, ladies."

Katelyn was taken aback. "Nat, it's like forty bucks. You don't need to do that."

Nat tossed her card over. "I insist."

"Did I ever tell you how much I love you?" Katelyn tapped in the digits of Nat's card. "And just know this meal will sustain me for the next fifteen hours. I literally had to drink the burnt coffee at the hospital today because I couldn't swing paying for one at the cart on the corner."

"I hear you," Tatum said, running her fingers through her new banana curls as she climbed on the bed next to Nat. "I'm so broke these days. I've been treating myself to whatever I want since the breakup, and my bank account is feeling it."

Katelyn rolled her eyes. "Oh, come on, Tate. Your Everett paycheck puts my student stipend to shame."

"It's all relative. Your parents paid for your undergrad, but I take a $500 loan payment hit each month. Add that to this overpriced apartment and everything else in this city. I mean why didn't we decide to live in, like, Delaware, where the cocktails aren't $24?"

Tatum tried to make a joke of it, but deep down she knew Katelyn's finances were probably a whole lot messier than hers.

"Um, because Delaware sucks and there's a reason no movie has ever been set there," Katelyn laughed, tapping the curler to see if it was still hot.

Nat was listening, but she pretended to be absorbed in her phone. Typically, she would have jumped right into the "help, I'm so broke" conversation, but since she'd started seeing Bill, money just wasn't an issue.

She felt like she had more money than she knew what to do with. But it also felt like a dirty little secret. She didn't want to splurge on anything too extravagant for fear she'd be found out. She couldn't even fathom her friends' (or God forbid her mother's) reactions if they found out she was accepting money to be at the beck and call of some random decrepit billionaire.

Of course, she *would* tell her friends, and soon. But with Katelyn constantly complaining about how she was going to pay for her next meal, and Tatum putting in long hours at the firm to earn every penny of overtime, she somehow couldn't stomach telling them this old guy was giving her cash. For now, she'd just buy them Chipotle.

"Enough about money; it's depressing me," Nat sighed, getting off the bed and going to Katelyn, who was struggling with the curler. She sat behind her friend, taking the wand from her hand and twirling Katelyn's silky black hair around the thick barrel. "You're going to be a vixen tonight! Let's get you A MAN."

"I second that; I need a man too. Let's go get *all* the single men in New York City —and maybe some not-single men as well!" Tatum snuggled back into a mound of pillows on the bed. "I can't believe Nat is the one with a boyfriend tonight." She picked up Katelyn's phone to track the status of their food delivery.

"I know! Speaking of the dentist, will he be making an appearance tonight?" Katelyn asked, checking her friend's reflection in the floor-length mirror. Nat's face turned bright red.

"Oooooh he is, isn't he!" Katelyn howled.

Nat cleared her throat. "First, he's not my boyfriend. We're still figuring out our love affair. Second, I don't think I can come out with you guys tonight," she finished, preparing for the blowback.

"What are you *talking* about? This has been the plan all week!" Katelyn jerked her head away from the curler, her tone disappointed and irritated.

"I know, I know. I totally planned on coming the whole time. It's just that JP texted me and he wants to try this new beer garden. I really haven't seen him this week with getting ready for Paris and everything. I'll definitely come out later, just keep me posted where you guys are." Nat's face looked pained, but really, she was just hoping her friends would buy her excuse.

"No, I get it. Come on Katelyn, she just started seeing this guy and she's excited! You know what that's like," Tatum remarked, coming to Nat's defense despite her own feelings of resentment.

"I PROMISE I will come to meet you guys after!" Nat pleaded with Katelyn as she glared at her in the mirror.

"Ugh. FINE. But only because you've been single for a long time and I support you venturing into this new relationship," Katelyn grumbled. "*And* because you bought me my Chipotle." Nat smiled back at Katelyn, which they both knew was her way of saying thank you.

Damn.

Nat was flooded with guilt. Even though JP *did* ask her to go to a beer garden, she'd had to cancel on him when Bill texted, requiring her presence at a scotch tasting. This sugar baby thing was turning out to be more of a commitment than she'd anticipated.

■ ■ ■

Nat stood outside her apartment building as she waited for Bill's familiar black Mercedes to pull up. He'd messaged her while she was still at Tatum's, telling her he wanted to take her shopping so she could look her "very best" at the Hamptons scotch tasting that evening.

What Nat *really* wanted to do was spend Saturday night with her friends, drink too many vodka sodas and go home with JP. But alas, Bill had to be her number-one priority if she wanted to stay on his payroll, which she did.

They had only seen each other twice, and both occasions had been more than tolerable. Their first encounter was the evening of the ballet, when the pair met at Eleven Madison Park, one of the city's premier fine dining restaurants in the Flatiron District. The spot was probably cool in the '90s, but in modern NYC it felt a little tired and extremely expensive, just like Bill.

Wearing the same red dress she'd shown off in her profile picture, Nat downed nearly an entire bottle of wine to calm her nerves before leaving the apartment to meet Bill at the restaurant. When she got there in her Uber, Bill met her out front. A hostess showed them to the VIP section, where they sat down in an Art Deco booth.

Even though everything on the tasting menu was foreign to Nat—something she would never dare admit to her prestigious company—she quickly found herself sampling what the evening had to offer. Foie gras seared with celtuce and radicchio. A parade of dishes featuring spring lamb, caviar, steelhead trout, and a gooey *Saint Félicien* cheese. And, to her surprise, mature conversation with Bill—more mature than those with any guy she'd ever dated.

His drawn-out speeches about entrepreneurship, sprinkled with advice for Nat on how to "get what she wants" were far more compelling than the "how was your day" routine from lazy suitors in her past. Sure, Bill fancied himself to be the most distinguished version of the American Dream—*how could he not?*

And he did over-use cringe phrases from the '70s, calling former colleagues "far out" and "real cool cats," but Nat found herself kind of *enjoying* her time with Bill. After a two-hour dinner and a lot of career talk, Bill took Nat to the ballet as promised. Of course, the two had a private box, and aside from a sly hand rubbing up against her thigh after intermission, the rest of the night proved uneventful.

Their second "date" was a fundraising gala for some charity where Bill served on the board. Much like the first time, they went to an extravagant dinner, followed by drinks, and ended the night at the gala. This time, Nat could *feel* his power.

Being a billionaire placed Bill in a league of his own. When they arrived at the gala they were led to the most exclusive table. Bill demanded a 23-year-old Pappy Van Winkle bourbon. Nat later learned, while frantically Googling in the bathroom, that the bottles cost $8,000. From the way people scurried to carry out his commands, Bill was clearly used to getting what he wanted, no questions asked.

Which is why when he leaned in for a handsy kiss with Nat in the backseat on the way home, she figured one small smooch (and a tit caress) wouldn't hurt. After all, aside from the occasional lingering stare or subtle ass graze, he'd behaved like a perfect gentleman. But now she couldn't help but cringe at the memory of his cracked lips and stale breath.

God, he even smelled like old man.

Their arrangement was a casual one. Bill would text her at the beginning of the week with the times and events for which he wanted her to be available. If she accepted, he would "incentivize" her to wear something nice with a healthy Venmo transfer, which subsequently locked her into the obligation. Last-minute meetings, such as the pre-scotch tasting shopping trip, were completely at Nat's discretion.

This, however, was the first time Bill had offered to pick Nat up. She didn't see this gesture as a reason for concern, since he'd dropped her off several times. More importantly, however, she didn't want to scuff the bottoms of her new black strappy, mini-platform Louboutins on the subway. Nat watched as the black Mercedes Benz SUV pulled up to the front of her building, and Marco the driver got out.

"Good afternoon, Natalie," he greeted her, coming around to open the door.

"Good afternoon, Marco, thank you for scooping me," she replied as she carefully stepped into the car. Bill was waiting, sipping an espresso. He wore a charcoal Armani suit with a jaunty red Hermès pocket square tucked in the breast pocket. His white hair was gelled in a comb-over, and the middle button of his jacket pulled at the fine Italian wool to accommodate his protruding stomach. Bill was by no means a "good looking" elderly man, but he tried his best with $10,000 suits and a different Rolex every day.

"Hello, beautiful," he said, as she took a seat in the farthest spot from him.

"Well, Bill, don't you look nice." She tried her best to sound genuine. "Thanks for messaging me. I'm excited about the scotch tasting tonight." It was the best lie she could manage as she adjusted her pleather pencil skirt that was rubbing against the leather seats.

"Well, we need to make sure you're as stunning as can be," Bill said between espresso sips, "so I took the liberty of booking an appointment with Celeste, my stylist at Bergdorf Goodman. I already sent her your measurements, so she's waiting for us with options at the store." He flashed her a big veneer-laden grin.

Wait, how did he get my measurements?

Nat remembered that was one of the questions she'd filled out for her Just Companions profile, but it still made her feel uneasy.

"Move closer to me," Bill commanded, patting the expanse of leather that separated them.

Um, do I have to?

Nat forced a smile and scooted over. She smelled his sour espresso breath when he reached across, putting his small, oddly soft hand on her right leg.

"Much better," he said with a toothy smile.

■ ■ ■

Nat's eyes widened when she saw the racks and racks of designer dresses, jackets, and accessories in the massive private room Bill had booked for their personal shopping appointment. The walls were lined in cream-colored leather, accented by plush ivory couches draped with beige cashmere throws. A heavy gold-framed mirror consumed one of the walls. The lighting, bright but not harsh, softened the curves of the golden Jonathan Adler vase on the low marble coffee table. A thin rose gold tray held a single white orchid, a frosty bottle in an ice bucket, and two delicate crystal flutes. Frank Sinatra crooned softly in the background.

Bill's request for sure.

"Champagne?" he asked, as Nat ran her fingers across the Balenciaga raw silk corset. She took in the perfectly tailored Bottega Venetta gown, slit to the thigh. Nearby, a rich maroon cowl neck top, clung to hanger with nothing but a fine tie at the neck.

"Sounds lovely," she said, accepting the flute of Dom Perignon. A sixtyish woman with a coiffed silver updo and a black power suit entered the large, mirrored room.

"*Bill,* darling. *How are* you?" she exclaimed, giving him a double-cheek air kiss. Her bold red lipstick left a faint stain on his crinkled cheek.

Celeste.

"And you must be *Natalie,*" she purred, not bothering to extend her hand. Nat heard the judgment in the woman's voice and experienced a twinge of insecurity.

How many young, bright-eyed girls had Bill dragged in here before? How many racks of size two dresses had she prepared for his past "dates?"

Nat couldn't help but feel self-conscious in front of the woman, as if they both knew how low she had stooped.

"Hi. Yes, I'm Natalie, but everyone calls me Nat." She knew her friendly nickname only emphasized her youth.

"She'll be going by Natalie," Bill said.

Nat immediately felt uncomfortable.

What, I can't pick my own name now?

Suddenly she wanted to be anywhere but there, regardless of all the luxury clothing he was buying for her. But before she could think of a reason to leave, she remembered that even if she exited right that second, she would still have to see Bill in a few hours for the scotch tasting in the Hamptons. He'd already Venmoed her money, which meant, per their agreement, she was contractually bound to go. She had already moved some of the money so she could pay her rent on time.

Okay, suck it up for a few more hours and you can be done for good. Try on custom couture pieces. How painful could that be?

"Shall we get started?" Celeste interjected, studying the clothes arrayed on the rack. "Why don't we try this first," she suggested, pulling out a backless lavender halter dress.

"An enchanting choice," Bill said, relaxing on the cream couch with another glass of champagne. Celeste beckoned to Nat, and she followed the older woman to a round pedestal in the corner of the room. A high, écru linen curtain created a small dressing room. Nat stepped onto the platform as Celeste hung the dress on a knob inside. Nat pulled the curtain shut and looked in the wall-mounted mirror inside her small sanctuary.

"Don't forget to smile when you come out," she heard Bill say, as he exchanged whispered comments with Celeste.

Breathe, Nat. Put the thing on, walk out there, and get this over with.

Sliding into the dress, she felt the fine silk glide over her body as she fumbled with the side zipper. Nat looked in the mirror, admiring herself in the glowing folds of liquid lavender. The color made her brown eyes pop.

If JP saw me in this, he would die.

She slid open the heavy curtain, stepped off the pedestal and executed a twirl as she made her way over to Bill.

"Natalie, you look stunning," he pronounced, still sunk into the couch. Nat could feel the heat from Celeste's stare. She stood in the corner, arms folded across her chest.

"Aw, thank you! I think this is perfect for tonight. What do *you* think?" Nat replied in her most girlie tone, hoping Bill would agree.

If he likes this one, we can call it a day.

"Slow down. We just got here. I think I'd like to see you in some other options," he said, while Nat stifled a sigh of disappointment. "Celeste, let's do the strapless Givenchy."

The woman hurried to the rack and pulled a fitted white wrap dress with delicate boning that would undoubtedly emphasize Nat's narrow waist.

"Yes, I want to see that on her," Bill nodded, talking about Nat like she wasn't even in the room.

That's when it hit Nat.

I'm his puppet. He's just playing dress-up with me, and I'm his little doll.

Nat grabbed the dress from Celeste's hand while giving her a robotic smile. "Sure Bill, I'll be right out," she agreed, her girlie tone starting to fade. She turned back to the dressing room.

How does he even know what Givenchy is?

Nat yanked the curtain closed as she hurried to change into the next ensemble. In a matter of seconds, she'd squirmed into the white dress and again descended from the pedestal, opening the curtain, and stepping into the mirrored room.

"I think we found a winner." Bill stood up from the couch. "This is my favorite. The white looks so...pure," he licked his lips, his watery gaze locked on Nat's body. Celeste discreetly rolled her eyes.

Nat felt mildly nauseous.

Ew. Pure? What a creep.

"Great! I love this one too; I think it's perfect. I think that means we're all set here? I still need time to get ready at my place before tonight so we'd better go," she burbled, hoping Bill would agree and they could be on their way. Nat was getting tired of Celeste's disapproval and Bill's leering insinuations.

"There's just *one more thing* I'd like to see on you." Bill spoke in a low voice as he made his way to the last rack. He browsed through the pieces, sliding the hangers across the sleek metal before pulling one out.

He turned. In his hand, Bill held a lacy black lingerie. Nat's stomach dropped.

You've got to be kidding me.

"Wow," Nat said, unsure of what to do next. "I mean, it's beautiful, but I don't think it would go with this look." She glanced down at her white dress.

He just said I looked pure. What the hell is he doing?

"No, of course not. But it would be a lovely addition to any woman's wardrobe. I just want to see you in it this once. After that, you can wear it for whomever, whenever you like." Bill extended his arm magnanimously, the underwear dangling from the hanger.

Nat ignored the knot in her stomach. She reached out her hand, feeling Bill's eyes on her as she examined the lingerie. It was a bra and panty set with a garter; the intricate black seams reminiscent of a high-end S&M dungeon. A network of narrow black straps held up the sheer lacey balconette bra. The barely-there thong was crafted from a black embroidered butterfly over invisible sheer tulle.

Without a word, Nat took the lingerie and made her way back to the linen curtain. Once inside, she slid off the Givenchy dress and stood there naked, analyzing the Agent Provocateur lingerie in front of her. It *was* beautiful. The elegant lace detailing along the edge of the bra and the fine silk stitching made the cheap red corset her friends bought her for her 21st birthday seem pitiful.

Very carefully, Nat removed the lingerie from the hanger and checked the price tag. *Seven hundred dollars.* Knowing she would change her mind if she thought about it too long, she closed her eyes for a second before stepping into the garments.

Holy shit.

She looked back at herself in the mirror, standing there clad in the stunning lingerie, looking more desirable than she'd ever dared to hope. The quality and design of the fabric made her body look feminine and voluptuous in just the right way. Nat felt undeniably sexy.

If only JP could see me now.

Mesmerized by her own reflection, Nat was feeling far less exposed than she thought she would. In fact, a new air of confidence came over her. She slipped on the new black Louboutins she'd worn earlier and admired herself once more in the mirror. She felt insatiable.

She drew back the heavy curtain and stepped out, striding once more into the mirrored room wearing nothing but the strappy lingerie and red-soled stilettos. She felt Bill and Celeste's stares on her skin and didn't care. Celeste fumbled with her clipboard, furiously propping her glasses atop her head.

Stare all you want, lady.

"So, Bill, what do you think?" Nat asked, whipping her hair to one side. Bill's mouth hung open, speechless, his eyes locked on her barely-clad curves.

"I think I like it," Nat said, her voice taking on a new confidence. "In fact, Celeste? It's Celeste, right? I'll take it in black and in any other colors you have."

Screw it. I look too good to feel insecure.

12

MAMMA MIA

"Have you been here before?" Nat asked as she slithered into the chair JP pulled out for her.

"No, I haven't. But I remember you saying you liked Greek food, so I thought it would be a nice place to try," he smiled as he took the seat across from her. "Plus, I wanted to show you off to all of Tribeca."

Nat bit her lip, flirting—half hoping she'd turn JP on—half hoping she could deflect since she didn't know how to respond to his compliment. She scanned the room—it was nothing like the lavish restaurants she had enjoyed with Bill.

Peeling light blue paint covered the wall and cracked decorative tiles lined the windowpanes. Traditional Greek guitar music strummed faintly in the background. The scene felt more like a poor man's Mamma Mia than the advertised "Restaurant Week" hotspot as noted by the *New York Times*.

"These hole-in-the-wall places always have the best food," Nat finally said. "Plus, I've been to like every Mediterranean place on the East side already."

"On all of your other dates?" JP glanced up from his menu.

"I only let them take me to Greek food if I *really* like them," she joked. Another deflection.

"Well, I mean, are you going on other dates? Like with other people? Because I'm not, I really…"

Shit. Are we really doing this right now?

"Good evening." Nat was relieved to see a curly-haired waiter appear at their corner table. "My name is Theo, and I will be helping you tonight. Can I get you both started with something to drink?" he asked, filling their chunky glassware with water from a carafe.

"Thank you," JP said before looking at Nat. "Ladies first. Nat, do you know what you want to drink?"

"Oh, yes." She swallowed and looked down at her menu for the first time, trying hard to mask her fluster from JP's earlier, not-so-subtle inquiry. "I'll just have a glass of the chardonnay, please." She smiled at the waiter and closed her menu.

"And for you, sir?"

"I'll have the same. And we'll start with the hummus and pita, I think." He looked nervously at Nat. "You like hummus, right? If you don't, we could order the feta dip thing, or whatever you want."

Nat smiled back, charmed by JP's unusual lack of cool.

Looks like I'm not the only one rattled by the near-relationship-defining chit-chat.

"The hummus is perfect."

"Sounds great. I'll be right back with that." Theo disappeared into the teeny kitchen, and Nat took a sip of her water.

"Sienna was really on one today. She's taken to wearing

sunglasses inside for extended periods of time. I think to make her feel more important?" Nat trailed off as she caught JP's gaze. His bright eyes smoldered as he tried to hide a playful smirk. "What?"

"Nothing." Now he was grinning. "You're just so cute when you talk about work." His hands extended across the table, gently folding his fingers into hers.

"You think I'm cute?" Nat pulled her hand from his and put her hair behind her ear.

"I think you're beautiful." JP's eyes hadn't moved from hers. "Listen, I've been wanting to talk to you about something." He brushed his fingers through his hair.

Good God, here we go again.

"My mom is coming into town from San Francisco next week. She does this annual girls trip to the City with her college room-mates. They make matching T-shirts and wear them on the plane. It's super-embarrassing. But anyway, she's coming a few days early to spend some time with me since I haven't been home in a while— you know with work and school coming up and everything."

Shit. Don't say it.

"Anyway, I mentioned I was starting to see someone, and you know how moms get, so anyway, I was hoping we—well the three of us—could all get dinner. She's great and she'd really like to meet you, and I think it would be great, and I know she would *love* you. But, of course, no pressure if you have plans or something." He tried his best to sound casual, running his fingers through his hair again.

"Oh." Nat swallowed harder this time. "You want me to meet your mom? Don't you think it's a little…soon?" She realized she was self-sabotaging again as the words came out of her mouth.

"Well, I know we've only been seeing each other for a couple of weeks, but she lives far away, and she isn't in the City often, so I just thought…you know what, don't worry about it." JP's smile tightened as he tapped his fingers on the rim of his water glass.

"I think it's too soon for all of that. Don't get me wrong, I do like spending time with you. I think we're having fun, you know? No need to rush into meeting the parents or anything serious." Nat immediately regretted sounding so cavalier.

Nobody has ever asked me to meet their parents. I can't believe I just blew him off. Of course, I want to meet your mom! But what if this fizzles out? What if I say something stupid and she convinces you to break up with me? If I meet her, would that mean we're actually dating, like officially?

"Just having fun, right." JP couldn't mask the disappointment in his tone.

"Two glasses of chardonnay."

Nat turned to see the familiar waiter wobbly place their drinks on the table, his (un)timely return acting as a buffer for the second time. "I'll be right back with that hummus," he added, darting away as quickly as he'd appeared.

Goddamnit Nat, what is wrong with you?!

13

AUDREY HEPBURN LIED

"It's Terminal 2," Sienna barked at the Uber driver while she furiously tapped out an email on her oversized iPhone. Nat winced.

This is going to be a long trip.

Sienna had already demanded the driver take the congested George Washington bridge, despite his GPS suggesting a quicker route, along with insisting he stop at a nearby Starbucks so she could get her third Americano of the day. And her imperious attitude was nowhere near letting up.

This work trip to Paris was something Nat had been looking forward to for the past four months. Transported by her vision of eating croissants near the Palais Royale while sporting a sassy red lip, Nat had a rude awakening when she learned that their 36-hour trip would be strictly business. Sienna had every minute planned out, from back-to-back client appointments, to order reviews and retail visits.

Nonetheless, Nat was excited. She hadn't been to Paris since she'd studied abroad in Florence and made an impromptu drunk weekend trip to France with her friends. There was something undeniably magical about traveling abroad, and Nat couldn't wait to get some perspective—especially since her work schedule and paltry paycheck made the possibility of booking her own European getaway a joke.

Just as the Uber driver was pulling up to JFK's Terminal 2, Nat felt her phone vibrate. She looked down to see a message from JP.

`I hope you have a safe flight Nat! I already can't wait to see you. I made a reservation for when you get back at that bistro you like on the corner of 26th and Park. Already thinking of all the ways I'm going to welcome you home...`

Nat blushed as JP's easy smile and kind eyes flashed through her head. Although she regretted turning down his maternal meet-and-greet, and despite the ongoing Bill situation, she liked him—a lot. Before JP, she'd spent the majority of her young adult life casually dating, trying not to be too vulnerable, and hooking up with a few guys since her move to the City. Right when she'd sworn off boys after being ghosted by yet another finance bro, JP had asked her out for a drink. After one cocktail turned into a romantic evening ferry ride to Brooklyn and a spontaneous trip to the movies, she had to admit he was different.

Is this what it's supposed to feel like?

JP was smart, funny, knew the sidewalk rule, and best of all—he was crazy about Nat. She looked down at her phone again and smiled.

`Let that imagination of yours run wild 😉. I'll text you when I land.`

"We're here; I hope you know our gate." Sienna snapped open the door and stepped out of the BMW.

"Gate G," Nat replied in her friendliest tone, thankful she'd already downloaded her boarding pass.

"There better be a bar close by; I need a drink." Sienna pulled her dark shades over her eyes. Nat shrugged and checked the time. Their flight wasn't taking off for another three hours.

She's probably more bearable if she's hammered anyway.

The two made their way into the airport. After an hour of checking bags and going through security, they found themselves at the bar of a seafood restaurant near Gate G.

"I'll take a double martini, dirty," Sienna ordered. The waiter seemed unfazed by her 10:30 AM request.

Guess it's just normal when you work in an airport.

"Natalie, what are you having?" Sienna asked.

"I'm actually okay with sparkling water for now," Nat told the waiter, as she dodged a sour look from Sienna.

"Sparkling water? Give yourself another five years and that'll be a vodka double," Sienna remarked. Nat didn't say anything. While part of her wanted to kill her boss, Nat couldn't help but feel bad for Sienna.

She was a disgruntled 35-year-old who'd worked her ass off for years in the fashion industry. And here she was, running around with someone nearly ten years her junior, making a measly $80K, and drinking cheap vodka in a busy airport. For the first time, Nat wondered if Sienna had started out just like her, with dreams of making a name for herself in the fashion world, only to end up selling clothes and bankrolling a lifestyle she could nowhere near afford.

"You've been working so hard to get ready for Paris. You deserve it!" Nat said, trying to appease her stressed-out boss.

"You have no idea." Sienna took a long sip from the potent drink the bartender set in front of her. "You know they told me I'd get Paris for Fashion Week," she continued, "and then out of the blue they decided they needed me in New York that week, so they sent me on this shitty showroom trip instead." Sienna sighed, and Nat could relate.

Who wouldn't be pissed off if they'd been promised a luxe Paris Fashion Week trip only to be bumped down to a bunch of client meetings, layover style?

"This is just as important if you ask me." Nat took a sip from her sparkling lime water. "I mean, handling orders and scheduling private appointments is really what makes Fashion Week even possible."

Sienna shot her a hard look. "The *least* they could have done is an upgrade to first class. I mean, an eight-hour flight in business? They'd better have enough liquor on board," she said with a cold laugh. Nat laughed with her for a moment before catching the attention of the bartender.

"You know what, I think I'll also do a martini," she said. "We might as well get a decent head start."

■ ■ ■

An exhausting eight hours later, Nat stepped out of the cab and took in the city around her.

Ahh, Paris.

She gazed in awe at the Parisians who were going about their lives, meeting up with friends, talking on their phones, and sipping nightcaps, all the while radiating that effortless elegance for which the City of Lights was famous. It helped her forget that brutal flight.

Sienna had called the attendant over five times to refill her glass, getting progressively louder and more demanding with every cocktail. Then there was that nightmare coughing baby behind her. Nat shook her head. None of that mattered now.

I'm in Paris! The Mecca of all things fashion!

"Bonjour, Bienvenue à Paris," the doorman greeted them, taking their bags as Nat stepped through the revolving door of the grand Relais Adrienne.

"Wow. It's so gorgeous," Nat breathed as she looked around at the gold detailing and decadent French aesthetic that embellished the luxurious lobby. Sienna beelined her way to the front desk, oblivious to the elegance. Nat jogged to catch up.

"We have two rooms under the name Sienna Quinn," Sienna said to the woman at the front desk, sounding somewhat pleasant for the first time since they took off.

Well, pleasant for Sienna.

"Bonsoir Madame," the woman greeted them, pausing a moment for the pleasantry to be returned. When Sienna just pursed her lips, making her frown lines look even deeper, the woman resumed typing at her computer. "Have you been to Paris before?" she eventually asked, her tone slightly chilly.

"Many times," Sienna replied, looking down at her phone.

So, Rude Sienna's back.

Feeling somewhat embarrassed by her boss's manners, Nat chimed in. *"J'adore Paris, j'ai fait quelques études ici."*

This wasn't entirely true, but she did have one too many glasses of champagne in Paris while she'd been studying in Italy, so it was kind of the same thing.

"Parfait! Vous parlez très bien français," the woman behind the desk

replied in her cheeriest voice yet. Sienna shot Nat a look that said she was profoundly unimpressed with Nat's language abilities.

The woman clicked her mouse and typed something. "Well, it seems one of the rooms has been upgraded."

"Oh, thank God," Sienna sighed, her tone perking up. She glanced over at Nat. "I'm sure we'll still be on the same floor, but it *does* make sense since I have the bulk of the work to do. They probably figured I need more space. Not to mention I *am* your boss, so it's the least they could do."

"Of course, it seems Mademoiselle Reardon has been upgraded to our most prestigious room, the Royal Suite," the woman continued, reading aloud from her screen.

Nat frowned, her face turning beet red.

What the hell is going on?

Sienna coughed. "I'm sorry, you said Natalie, but the upgrade is for Sienna Quinn, Q-U-I-N-N." She clenched her iPhone in her hands.

"Yes, Mademoiselle Quinn it seems you have booked a single room, and we have managed to get you a view of the river as you requested," the woman clarified, attempting to soothe the palpable tension in the air. Sienna tightened her jaw and adjusted her thick black glasses.

"As for you, Mademoiselle Reardon, your friend Bill is a very cherished client of ours. He has made a personal request that you receive the best accommodations, so do not hesitate to ask for anything."

Nat's stomach dropped.

How did I not see this coming?!

She had mentioned the name of the hotel to Bill when she'd had one too many scotches in the Hamptons, never thinking he would remember and upgrade her room to the Royal Suite! Normally, she'd relish the chance to stay in what was probably the most expensive room in Paris, but this was only driving even more of a wedge between her and Sienna. Not to mention undoubtedly stacking Bill's expectations upon her return.

Shit.

Nat tried to sound casual. "Oh, Bill, of course. Yes, he knows my parents really well. They must have mentioned to him that I was coming. How generous." She snuck a sideways look at Sienna, who still hadn't said a word. She didn't have to. Her eyes were like daggers in Nat's face.

"Look, I'm exhausted. We'll just take the keys to our rooms," Sienna snapped.

"Of course," the woman said, placing two room keys on the counter in front of them. Sienna quickly snatched hers.

"We'll meet down here at 8 AM *sharp*," she ordered Nat, making her way to the elevator.

"Okay, sounds good. Have a good night!" Nat took her room key from the counter. *"Merci,"* she said to the woman as she turned to make her way to the elevators.

She really hates me now.

■ ■ ■

"Just use the smart screen by the door if you wish to call the concierge. Your butler, Pierre, will tend to your requests without delay," a well-dressed man explained. Nat was standing in the middle of the extravagant Royal Suite, gasping at the Belle-Epoque-meets-modern-Euro decadence of the 2,200-square-foot accommodation.

Reflective steel detailing adorned the exquisite four-tiered chandelier, engulfing the room in what looked like a patina of diamonds. Sheer damask fleur-de-lis silk curtains rippled in the breeze before the French doors that opened to a private balcony, a view of the glittering Eiffel Tower in plain sight.

Pure. French. Opulence. And all for ME!

"Oh. Um, yes. Thank you so much."

"Of course, Mademoiselle. Enjoy your visit to Paris." The man retreated, shutting the door behind him.

Nat just stood there, absorbing her lavish surroundings. This was another galaxy from the cheap hostel she'd booked with her friends the last time she was in this city. Unsure of what to explore first, she made her way over to the private balcony and stepped outside to admire the unbelievable view of the Eiffel Tower.

Nat stood with the cool night breeze wrapping around her, redolent of coffee, diesel, and exotic perfumes. *This* was the Paris she had always envisioned: romantic and spectacular.

Nat walked back inside and checked out the rest of her temporary Parisian home. She ran her fingers across the gorgeous red tufted couch, her heels clicking on the marble floor. She admired a rococo portrait of Marie Antoinette mounted above the fireplace, noticing the fine strokes of oil paint and the thick giltwood frame, details that made the colossal painting convincing enough to be an original.

Shit, is it an original?

Just as Nat was about to take a seat on one of the upholstered chairs that matched the garnet velour Napoleon III-style sofa, something caught her eye. A bouquet of long-stemmed white roses and a bottle of 2012 Bollinger Pinot Noir Champagne rested atop the gilded coffee table. She walked over and picked up the card.

Natalie,
A beautiful city for a beautiful girl.
See you when you get back.

xBill

Nat looked down at the note, feeling ill. Nothing about this felt magical. It was transactional—and creepy. The note reminded her that to him, she was something that could be bought. Nat couldn't deny Bill's generosity, but they were using each other, and Bill invariably had the upper hand.

Suddenly, she felt angry he had found a way to insert himself into her personal life, and even worse—into her work. To her, he served one purpose—and he had no business involving himself in the other aspects of who she was.

Furious and scared, Nat took out her cell phone and started typing.

Bill, I got the upgrade, and it was unnecessary. Our arrangement doesn't say anything about spontaneous and unexpected gifts.

She hit Send.

How dare he? Why does he think it's okay to manipulate my life like this?

Even worse, she couldn't help but blame herself for letting things get this far. It wasn't the Paris she'd dreamed about after all because she never thought she'd be there as the "companion" of a sugar daddy.

Initially, she'd thought she would stop accepting money and gifts from Bill once she got ahead on her rent and bought a few things for the trip, but as the gifts got more extravagant, Nat had lost sight of herself. Plus, she could tell Bill was getting restless.

First the handsy kiss, then the lingerie fashion show, now this?

She couldn't help but wonder what Bill would be expecting in return when she arrived back in NYC. At this moment, she wanted nothing more than to be in a single, standard room like Sienna.

She walked to the bedroom and collapsed on the buttery soft Egyptian cotton sheets that cloaked the king-sized canopied bed. She rested her head on one of the twelve decorative velvet pillows behind her. Then she remembered she had a message from the girls in her voicemail—she'd seen it when they landed, but she'd waited to check it until she was out of Sienna's sight. She put it on speaker and listened to Katelyn and Tatum:

"Hello, little Frenchie! We just wanted to call and make sure you landed safely, and we wanted to tell you that we are soooo proud of you for chasing your dreams. We love you!"

Nat lay on the bed as she replayed the message, tears rolling down her cheeks. Why did she have to listen to Sienna and Poppy when they made it sound like she wasn't enough? Or her own self-doubt when it came to not only her work but her love life?

She had the most incredible friends, a cute guy who was falling for her, and a job that she was grateful to have. And she'd risked all that for what? To wear more designer clothes? Nat crawled under the feather duvet, the size of the massive bed making her feel even more alone, and lay sobbing, her wet face buried in the pillow.

Here she was in Paris, in the most beautiful hotel room she had ever seen, with a wardrobe she'd dreamt of owning her whole life—but all she really wanted to do was drink cheap wine in some Zara tank top, laughing with her girlfriends in her teeny apartment.

■ ■ ■

Nat's eyes adjusted to the sunlight blazing through the silk damask curtains. She rolled over and looked at the clock on the nightstand: 7:36 AM.

Shit!

She scrambled out of bed in a panic. She had 24 minutes before she had to meet Sienna in the lobby. Her plan to wake up early and blow dry her hair was completely derailed, and as she struggled to turn on the elaborate shower, she realized she hadn't even changed since getting off the plane.

Sienna's going to kill me if I look like shit.

Nat jumped under the scalding jets and reemerged minutes later. She would have to let her hair air dry.

So much for a sleek Parisian blowout.

Wrapping a fluffy white towel around her, Nat started damage control on her face, wasting no time in applying a thick layer of foundation followed by her signature smokey eye. Thankfully, she'd pre-planned her outfits so she wouldn't have to waste any more precious time.

She checked her phone, anxious to see if Sienna had already texted her that she was waiting in the lobby. There were two messages from her mom, a missed call from JP, and a message from Bill.

Bill.

Her heart raced at the thought of reading Bill's reply, thinking of the rage text she'd sent the night before.

I can't deal with this right now.

Nat threw her phone on the bed and rummaged through her suitcase, pulling out the clothing she'd planned for Day One. She threw on the black blazer dress and a thick gold-plated chain necklace as she slid into her Gucci snakeskin loafers. She checked herself one last time in the mirror as she applied the last of the NARS lip gloss she'd found at the bottom of her baby blue Miu Miu shoulder bag.

Not bad.

Nat smiled at herself, proud of her speedy makeover. She might have started out on the wrong foot, but she was determined to turn this Paris trip around.

Sienna wasn't sitting in the lobby with a scowl on her face, so Nat made her way to the espresso machine.

Guess I'm not the only one who overslept.

She filled two demitasse cups at the counter and walked back to the couch where they'd arranged to meet, figuring the espresso could act as a peace offering. Nat sipped the strong coffee, letting the familiar warmth course through her, hoping it would ease the slight headache she had from crying herself to sleep the night before. She checked her phone for the time: *8:07 AM.*

This is weird.

Sienna was usually so punctual, and she'd been explicitly clear with Nat that they were operating on a very tight schedule. Sienna had said their first appointment would be at 9 AM in an atelier located in the Marais, a fifteen-minute drive from the hotel. Nat decided she would wait just a few more minutes and took out her phone.

Bonjour! Hope you slept well. I'm down here in the lobby, just wanted to make sure we're still planning on meeting here and leaving together?

Nat hit send and stared at her screen, waiting for the familiar typing bubbles to appear.

Did this bitch leave without me? I know she was pissed about the upgrade, but that would be a new low, even for her.

Nat uncrossed her legs and began nervously tapping her foot, her eyes still locked on the screen. She tapped Sienna's contact and put the phone to her ear as the line began to ring.

Voicemail. Shit.

Just as Nat was about to call again, she glanced at the clock. *8:13.* She got up, adjusted her purse over her shoulder and made her way up to the front desk.

The same woman was behind the computer who had helped them only hours before. "Excuse me," Nat said, not in the mood to practice her French.

"*Bonjour Mademoiselle,* how can I help you?" The woman looked up from her screen.

"Hi. I don't know if you remember but you helped me, and another woman check in late last night. You haven't seen her by any chance, have you? She has big black glasses, blonde hair, super thin."

"Of course, I remember, Miss Quinn. She was anticipating the upgrade," the woman said. Nat flinched at the thought of their stressful check-in experience.

"Yes, that's her. Sienna Quinn."

"No Mademoiselle, I have not seen her since check-in last night." The woman began typing. "However, it does say here that she called the front desk last night for a wake-up call at 6 AM this morning."

What? 6 AM—that was two hours ago. What could she be doing?

"Okay, and do you remember which room she was staying in?"

"Yes, it seems she was in Room 412, facing the river."

"Great, *merci!*" Nat replied, walking briskly towards the elevator, tapping Sienna's contact once more.

Did she just oversleep? There's no way. Maybe she's on the phone with the client? Or did she rearrange the whole schedule and didn't tell me out of spite because of the Royal Suite thing?

Voicemail again. Nat stepped into the elevator, annoyed at the prospect of Sienna intentionally keeping her out of the loop. Regardless of why Sienna wasn't in the lobby when she said she would be, Nat deserved to know the plan. After all, this was her job too and she wasn't going to let her jealous superior make her look bad to the client or the label.

Nat stormed off the elevator in search of Room 412. It was a corner room at the end of the hallway, nothing like Nat's luxury setup. She walked to the door and pressed her ear up against it.

Nothing.

She thought maybe she would hear Sienna talking on the phone, or a hairdryer, but she didn't hear a thing. She checked her phone one last time. *8:29.* They had an appointment in just thirty minutes, and they still had to get to the atelier and prepare the looks and pricing sheets for the client.

Nat took a deep breath and slowly raised her hand, giving the door three hard knocks. She was prepared for Sienna to rip open the door and order her to wait outside, but still nothing. She leaned in to listen again. Then she knocked once more, this time harder, but still no movement on the other side of the door.

A maid walked out of the neighboring room.

Time for action.

"Hello, my mom took the only hotel key and left for the day, and I locked myself out and forgot my wallet," Nat explained in her most convincing lost-little-girl voice, the same one she often used for Bill. The woman looked at her blankly.

Shit, she doesn't speak English.

Nat tried again in her best broken French to repeat her lie to the cleaning woman, who by the grace of God either understood, felt bad, or couldn't be bothered—because without verifying her story, she reached over and unlocked the door before making her way to the next room.

"Merci beaucoup, c'est très gentil!" Nat said to the disinterested maid, but she was already gone.

Okay, she's probably going to fire me for this, but screw it.

Nat gripped the handle tightly as she stood in front of the open door. "Sienna? Good morning, it's me. I'm sure you changed the schedule and forgot to tell me but it's past 8:30 and we should really leave soon if we're going to be in the fourth arrondissement on time."

There was no answer.

"Sienna, are you in there?" Nat pushed at the door and saw the small room undisturbed, the bed still made from the night before. Tentatively, she entered. A pair of nude scuffed Louboutins were discarded by the door, and Sienna's open suitcase sat on a stand, her clothes neatly packed inside.

"Sienna?" Nat tried not to sound alarmed. Just when she was convinced Sienna couldn't be in the room, she heard the faint sound of moaning coming from the bathroom. She made her way over and pushed open the cracked bathroom door.

"Get me a drink," Sienna mumbled when she looked up and saw Nat standing in the doorway. Nat couldn't believe her eyes. Sienna was slumped over the toilet in a skintight red Mugler dress, her makeup running down her face. The overwhelming stench of vomit saturated the room.

"Um, yes. Okay," Nat stammered, in shock. She hurried to the fridge in the corner of the room and knelt by the minibar, where she now noticed ten empty vodka nips strewn across the floor. Nat grabbed a water bottle and rushed back to the bathroom, where she handed Sienna the water.

"Are you okay? Should I call someone?" Nat asked, hoping Sienna would tell her everything was going to be fine.

"I don't want *this*." Sienna burped as she carelessly tossed the water bottle behind her. "Isn't there any vodka left in here?"

Nat stared down at her boss. Her bloodshot eyes were glazed over, her skinny figure twisted over the toilet, reeking of booze. "Are you drunk?" Nat asked softly, still in shock.

Sienna laughed to herself before flinging her head back over the toilet to further empty the contents of her stomach, which apparently was exclusively vodka.

Nat started to panic.

I can't take her to the client like this. Think, Nat.

She turned on the shower and started unzipping the back of Sienna's dress. She had spent plenty of her college years sobering up drunk friends, never expecting the skill to come in handy when it came to her uptight, apparently alcoholic, boss.

"Get in the shower," Nat said in a firm voice. "I have to make a few phone calls." She couldn't believe this was happening. How was she going to explain to her superiors in New York that they had lost substantial clients?

Sorry you flew us all the way out to Paris where we lost a bunch of orders because Sienna's a raging booze hound.

"Boooo, no fun!" Sienna slurred, as she stood up to get in the steaming shower.

After getting the code from Sienna, Nat walked out of the

bathroom and took Sienna's phone from the small desk near the window. She had only met Sienna's boss once, back when she was first hired. Maria was a seasoned professional who intimated Nat just by being in the same room with her. Nat cringed as she remembered Sienna mentioning Maria was in Tokyo collaborating with the Vogue Japan team.

She scrolled through Sienna's contacts until she got to Maria's name. She stood there trying to think of another way to salvage the appointments, or at the very least her boss's reputation in the hopes of preserving their already strained relationship. She came up empty. With the client already waiting at the atelier, she brushed her thoughts of heroism aside and hit dial. As the line was ringing, Nat looked up at a framed print above the headboard. Audrey Hepburn's famous quote in big bold lettering, *"Paris is Always a Good Idea."*

"Liar," Nat muttered to herself.

A scratchy voice came through on the other end of the phone. "This better be good Quinn, it's three in the morning."

Yeah right, Audrey. This is the trip from hell.

14

I CAN'T BELIEVE THIS IS HAPPENING

"Wait, so you're telling me that you came home early because your boss was blackout drunk at eight in the morning and you couldn't make your meeting?" Katelyn asked in disbelief as she opened the small fridge and took out a can of zero-calorie root beer.

"It was a *nightmare*," Nat said, ensconced in the fluffy Papasan chair that took up half of Katelyn's minuscule living room. "And as if that wasn't bad enough, the whole plane ride back she wouldn't even look at me. It was *so* awkward."

"I mean, kind of iconic on her part," Katelyn joked, flopping on her outstretched bed next to Tatum.

"She must have gotten fired for that," Tatum added, scrolling Katelyn's laptop for a binge-worthy Netflix show.

"I would assume so. Her boss was FURIOUS. Like I could tell she was fuming, but she said she'd take care of the client and that we had to get on the next flight back to New York as soon as Sienna felt better. I was literally still jet-lagged from the flight there when we got to the airport. *Such* a shit-show."

Nat had to laugh, thinking of the absurdity of her 24 hours in Paris. "Kind of tragic really. I mean, thinking back I should have seen the signs, I just never thought someone so outwardly put together was a raging alcoholic."

"I feel sorry for her. She was probably so embarrassed. If I were her, I'd have been looking up treatment centers the whole flight back." Tatum settled on a low-budget crime documentary that she tried to Airplay on Katelyn's Apple TV. "Well, we're glad you're back! It was a long day and a half without you."

"I wish I could say it was incredible and I wish you guys were there with me but I'm just grateful to be back in this shitty walk-up—and that I still have my job," Nat smiled, sipping on her milky iced coffee.

"Well, in other news, I think I have a date tonight," Tatum said, looking up from the laptop.

"OH MY GOD. WHAT?!" Nat screamed, dropping her phone in her lap.

"When? With who? Do we know him? Can we see a picture?" Katelyn jolted up from the bed, nearly spilling her can of soda.

Tatum put her head down to cover her blush. "His name is Luke and I met him at work," she said, feeling a mix of guilt and self-consciousness about her telling her friends the half-truth. "You guys, it's not a big deal, we're just two adults going to get dinner," she added in her best breezy voice.

Tatum looked at Nat, then at Katelyn. The truth was, she *wasn't* going to grab a bite with her new colleague Luke that evening—she had plans to watch a movie with Lola. After their awkward *misunderstanding* a few weeks earlier, Tatum had reached out to apologize and offered a movie night as a last-ditch effort to smooth things over. At least that's what she told herself. She still wasn't sure what her intentions were with Lola, or even what she would do when she saw her. All she knew was, she had to see her again.

"Tate, this IS a big deal. I mean, you haven't been on a date since you-know-who," Katelyn insisted, calling attention to the elephant in the room named Blake.

Tatum looked up, her face still red. "Yeah, I know, but it's time. I mean we broke up and I need to put myself out there." She felt the same knot in her stomach she always did when she spoke about Blake.

"Well, I for one am proud of you *and* your growth." Nat beamed at Tatum. "I'm shocked the whole unexpected lesbian come-on thing didn't make you want to crawl into your apartment and never resurface in the dating scene. I was shook just hearing about it."

Tatum quickly looked down. "Yeah! That experience was definitely a shocker."

"Well JP and I are going to a movie tonight, I think. The four of us should meet up for a drink after if things are going well," Nat suggested. "And Katelyn, obviously you should come too. You don't need to bring a date; you're fabulous on your own—unless sexy med student has finally come to his senses?"

"No, I'm so tired. All I've wanted to do lately is relax," Katelyn yawned, deflecting the comment about Peter, who she hadn't seen or heard from since his disappearing act at the hospital. "Plus, I spent so much money this weekend I need to chill below the poverty line for a bit." She wiggled her way under the covers.

"Sounds fair," Tatum said, before turning back to Nat. "So, what should I wear tonight? I'm going to post a pre-date thirst trap, so Blake sees it and wants to die."

"Well, I just so happen to have all these fabulous clothes from a Paris trip that never happened, so I'm sure we can find something. And with that face, it won't be hard to turn up the heat!" Nat leapt off the Papasan chair and climbed into bed with her friends.

■ ■ ■

So. Fucking. Hot.

Katelyn typed in Just Us Girls, responding to the smoldering selfie that Tatum sent to the group. She put her phone face-down on the counter. The girls had left several hours earlier to get ready for their respective date nights. They'd tried to convince Katelyn to join them, but she was already happily committed to an uneventful night in.

While Katelyn was happy for Tatum, knowing she hadn't been on a date since Blake took her to a college pizza joint more than five years before, she couldn't help but mask her definite jealousy. She knew Tatum was nervous and excited, and probably also a little sad, and Katelyn wanted to be there for her. But she still felt jealous of her gorgeous blonde friend—and she hated herself for it. Everyone always hit on Tatum. At bars, at supermarkets, on the streets—and not just creeps. Good-looking men were always asking for her number, sending her flowers, buying her drinks—even Tatum herself couldn't deny the effect she had on men.

Meanwhile Katelyn got plenty of men to go home with her, but they never seemed to take her seriously. By now she'd convinced herself that she didn't want to be "girlfriend material," anyway.

Of course, Tatum is fresh off a five-year relationship and lands her first date in years with some sexpot financial analyst whose parents probably have a summer house in the Hamptons. And I'm over here unable to hold the attention of a selfish prick med student for more than a couple of weeks.

She knew her feelings toward Tatum were unfair. She wanted so badly to suppress them, but no matter how hard she tried, she couldn't ease the sting of rejection. Tatum's blossoming love life seemed like a constant reminder of her own stagnant one.

Katelyn stared around her tiny kitchen before deciding that a crying session over some green tea and *The Notebook* would be the cure-all to her crappy mood. She filled the electric kettle and threw her hair into a messy bun.

Who needs a date when I can watch Noah and Ali make out in the rain for three hours and then die peacefully in their sleep together?

She reached for the mint-infused Trader Joe's tea. As she waited for the water to boil, she went into her small bathroom in search of the cheap face mask she knew she'd buried somewhere. She opened the mirrored cabinet, which revealed a small shelf holding her toothpaste and a hairbrush—but no mask. She knelt under the sink and opened the cabinet door.

I know I have it in here somewhere.

She rummaged through the toilet paper rolls, tampons, and boxes of miscellaneous beauty supplies before coming across a blue and white box she didn't recognize. Pulling it out of the cabinet, she realized it was the pregnancy test Tatum had forced her to buy a few months earlier when she'd convinced herself she and Blake were expecting, only to be brought back to reality with a late period.

Katelyn examined the box. She kind of wanted to take it.

What's the harm, you're not pregnant. Anyway, it's here and you might as well.

Then her stomach twisted. She *had* been abnormally tired recently. She cried every other night, which was totally out of character. Then she remembered thinking she was late, only to be relieved when she'd gotten a light period a week before.

She tore open the package and sat down on the toilet.

I'm just going to do this for peace of mind.

Once she was finished, Katelyn put the stick on the counter and grabbed the box from the floor.

Get accurate results in just three minutes!

She read the back of the box.

One line, not pregnant; two lines, pregnant.

She stood up from the toilet and started nervously rearranging her beauty products. She felt like her heart was going to beat out of her chest. She hadn't been on birth control since the hormones had made her depressed in college, but she was also sure she'd gotten her period since sleeping with Peter, who'd insisted they forgo a condom.

Katelyn looked down at the test.

Still nothing.

She went into the kitchen. Her hand shook when she poured the tea she'd craved only minutes before. Suddenly the thought of ingesting anything at all made her feel sick. She watched the clock on her phone as one minute went by. Then two, and finally three.

Katelyn slowly slunk back to the bathroom, shutting the door behind her despite being alone in the apartment. She took a deep breath, reiterating *you're fine* in her head as she looked down at the white stick sitting on the edge of the sink. Her body felt numb as she stood frozen, her eyes locked on the two dark pink lines, their significance immediately registering in her mind.

Pregnant.

■ ■ ■

Katelyn was unsure how long she'd been sitting on the bathroom floor. She figured it must have been a few hours when she heard her phone ringing from the kitchen. She'd forgotten Tatum planned to call with an update after her date with Luke.

When she tried to get up on shaking knees Katelyn had to use the toilet as support. Once on her feet, she avoided looking in the mirror at all costs. She wasn't ready to see herself yet, a stranger in her own body.

On her way out of the bathroom, she caught another glimpse of the pregnancy test on the edge of the sink. Still two pink lines.

Still pregnant.

She walked over to where she'd left her phone on the counter when she was blissfully unaware of her condition. As expected, Tatum was calling. Katelyn answered and put the phone to her ear.

"Kate? Are you there? I'm just leaving the restaurant now—he was cute, but I don't think I'm that into it. I couldn't stop thinking about Blake."

Tatum, couldn't tell the truth—that she and Lola sat through almost thirty minutes of a Lifetime movie before Lola admitted she had no interest in seriously pursuing Tatum, even though Tatum was "mind-bendingly hot." Lola explained she was committed to her boyfriend. Tatum was shocked to realize she felt relieved, but also weirdly disappointed.

"Tate," was all Katelyn could say, her voice cracking.

"Katelyn, what's wrong? You sound scared."

Without hesitating, Katelyn said, "I'm pregnant."

It was the first time she'd said the words out loud. They sounded even more severe than she'd expected. Hearing herself say that phrase made it real.

Holy shit, I'm pregnant.

Tatum was silent for a few seconds. "Don't move. I'm coming over."

Without saying anything else, Katelyn hung up her phone and dropped it on the counter. She put her head in her hands and for the first time since seeing the double pink lines, she felt something other than pure shock—fear.

■ ■ ■

Katelyn was jerked from her thoughts by a knock at her door. "It's me, open up!"

Tatum.

Had she made her way uptown in record time, or had Katelyn's concept of time morphed yet again?

She opened the door and Tatum burst in. "Hi! Oh my God!" She threw her arms around Katelyn and the two of them stood there, hugging.

"How? When did this happen? Are you sure?" Tatum finally loosened her grip.

"Tatum. I don't know. I don't know what to do," Katelyn finally said, her eyes filling with tears. "I can't believe this is happening. What do I *do*?" she moaned, her sniffle progressing into a loud bawl.

"We're going to figure this out together. Breathe. It's going to be okay," Tatum insisted, trying desperately to comfort her hysterical friend while leading the way inside the matchbox apartment to the teeny bed-couch. "We're going to get through this. You're not alone." She started rubbing Katelyn's back, causing Katelyn to weep even harder.

After a few minutes, Katelyn sniffed loudly and wiped the tears from her eyes. "Oh my God. What am I going to *do*? I can't tell my mom. I can't tell Peter. I don't have any money. Oh My God, this *can't be happening.*"

"Okay, ssshhh. We're going to lay all our options out on the table and I'm going to be here with you the whole time," Tatum instructed as she took out her phone. She knew Nat was in a movie with JP, but she sent her an emergency text anyway. Their friend needed all the support she could get right now. Katelyn sat down on the small stool at the counter while Tatum made her way towards the stove.

"I'm going to make us some tea and you're going to tell me everything," Tatum said in her most calming voice. Katelyn tried to speak but was too frantic to form a cohesive thought. Tatum reached across the counter and grabbed her hands. "It's okay, breathe. If there's ever a time for Nat's Meditation Masterclass B.S, this is it."

Katelyn looked up at Tatum and took a deep breath in through her nose as she closed her eyes, tears rolling down her face. She took several deeper breaths and tried to shut out the rest of the world.

Just breathe Kate, just breathe.

Finally, she gained enough self-control to speak. "I can't believe this is happening," she said for the third time. "Everything feels so surreal."

"I know. But you need to stay calm so we can talk through it all and figure out the best course of action," Tatum said. Her big blue eyes locked on Katelyn's. "I'm not going anywhere."

Katelyn took another slow breath. "It's Peter's."

"Okay," Tatum responded, her voice as comforting and calm as she'd promised.

"We didn't use a condom when he came over. I mean, I guess I knew it could happen. How could I be so *stupid?*" Katelyn's voice quivered.

"Stop. We're not doing this. We've all had sex without condoms at one point or another and we all knew what the consequences could be. We're past that. We're not going to harp on it. There's nothing we can do about the condom now." Tatum's voice was still calm, but her tone was firmer. There was no point in lamenting over the things neither she nor Katelyn could change. They had to commit to dealing with the fact that Katelyn, at this moment, was pregnant. Condom or not.

"Shit you're right," Katelyn said, regaining her composure. "I have to get an abortion." She darted a glance at Tatum, looking for confirmation.

"If that's what you want to do then that's what we'll do," Tatum replied, turning to switch on the kettle.

"Tate. I *have* to get an abortion, right? I can't have a baby." Katelyn was desperate for Tatum to make the decision for her.

This can't be happening.

"Can I even *get* an abortion, like legally?"

Her voice cracked as she stared at her friend, whose face had turned pale. Katelyn's brain cut to the busy pro-life protest she'd be-grudgingly walked through in Union Square Park the week before.

Images of "Baby Killer" posters littered with graphic depictions of bloody fetuses flooded her memory.

"I think I'm going to be sick."

Tatum poured two cups of green tea and walked around the small island to sit on the stool next to Katelyn. "Listen to me. I will support you in whatever you want to do. If you want to get an abortion, we can make an appointment at Planned Parenthood. Luckily, here in New York, abortions are still legal and safe, so if there's one thing to be grateful for, it's that. Or if you want to have a baby, I'll make a freaking registry at Babies 'R' Us. You don't have to make a decision right now; you can think about it. You *need* to think about it."

Katelyn wiped the tears from her cheeks then took the hot tea in her hands. She took a sip to try and soothe her stomach

I can't have a baby.

Tatum knew what she was about to say would exacerbate Katelyn's emotions, but it was an important part of figuring their way out of this— the first decision Katelyn had to make. She asked, "Are you going to tell Peter?"

The knot in Katelyn's stomach tightened.

"How can I? We haven't spoken since he was over here weeks ago. Then that whole thing in the hospital. He doesn't even want to look at me! How can I tell him I'm pregnant with his child?" she wailed.

Katelyn had been so numb from the pregnancy revelation that Peter hadn't really crossed her mind until now. "No," she said, "I'm doing this alone. I don't want him to know. I don't want *anyone* to know," she finished, taking another sip of her piping hot tea before looking down. "I have *no money*."

Tatum knew she didn't have any money. There wasn't a time in the past two years when Katelyn *hadn't* complained about money. She was financing her way through PA school with loans. She worked her ass off just to cover rent and groceries until her student loan refund kicked in. Her suffocating financial situation was anything but a secret to her friends.

"I'll help you. Don't worry about money."

Katelyn broke down in sobs, pushing her tea aside and laying her head on the cold counter in front of her.

Tatum's phone buzzed. Looking down, she saw that Nat had messaged her, surely having seen Tatum's "get to Katelyn's now" text. Tatum checked her phone:

```
Nat: What?
Nat: What's going on?
Tatum: Just come over!
Nat: Is everything ok?
Nat: Ok, coming
Tatum: We'll explain when you get here
```

Tatum tucked her phone away in the pocket of her oversized cardigan, feeling pained as she watched her friend cry. "Nat's coming over," was all she could offer.

Katelyn was usually the one who knew exactly what to say, and at this moment Tatum did not. She empathized with Katelyn's pain, but there was no way she could understand her inner turmoil. Her friend's world had crashed down around her, and Tatum felt horrible.

Katelyn lifted her head. "I need to go to Planned Parenthood this week."

"Are you sure? You have time."

"I'm getting an abortion. I can't have a fucking kid; I don't have a choice." Katelyn tried her best to sound sure. "My weekly grocery budget is $50. I'm so poor! Oh my God. If my *mom* found out?" Her eyes widened with fear.

"I'll make an appointment this week," Tatum said, trying for a reassuring smile. "I'll front the money. I was saving for a vacation with Blake and we all know that's not happening. Plus, I have a little emergency fund I set aside when I was still living at home. It's going to be okay."

Katelyn got up from the stool and ran to the sink. "I'm going to be sick."

Her heart pounded in her chest. Her body felt stiff. The reality of her pregnancy sank in. She hurled her chest over the sink and retched, beads of sweat forming on her forehead.

Tatum rushed to her. "If you're sure you want to do this, I'll call in the morning. The sooner we make an appointment, the sooner we can put all this behind us."

Katelyn nodded, running the water and swiping at her mouth with a paper towel. "What if it was a false positive?" she asked, with a twinge of hope.

"As much as I would love that for you, I think those are a myth."

Tatum didn't want Katelyn getting her hopes up for a miracle. "But, I'm sure they re-test you when you get to the clinic. If it was a false positive, we'll know for sure when we get there."

Retreating to the stool, Katelyn tried to mask her despair with humor. "Who would have guessed my Memorial-Day-Weekend bout of chlamydia would be the least of my slutty consequences?"

As she intended, Tatum laughed. Katelyn's intro to STDs came when she'd hooked up with some sophomore in college after one too many shooters on Memorial Day weekend. Even though both Katelyn and Tatum wished a seven-day Z-pack could make a baby go away, both girls knew if Katelyn was already cracking jokes, everything would eventually be okay.

■ ■ ■

Katelyn lay in her bed staring at the ceiling. The sirens of the City whining through the window kept pace with her racing thoughts. She turned on her side and grabbed her phone from the nightstand, trying not to wake the sleeping Tatum nestled beside her. She looked at the screen, 1:39 AM.

Nearly four and a half hours had passed since she'd taken the test, and Katelyn still couldn't wrap her head around her new reality. It was also nearly four and a half hours before she had to be up for work.

Work. Kill me. Work means Peter. Peter. Fuck.

She tapped to her messages and then to Peter's name.

We need to talk.

She stared at the message and frantically backspaced. Katelyn paused for a minute that felt like a lifetime before she began typing once more.

I'm pregnant.

Just rip the Band-Aid off, Katelyn. He should know he's the one who impregnated me with his seed on a worn-out fucking Murphy bed.

Before she could change her mind again, she hit Send and put her phone faced own on the nightstand. She pulled the covers up tight as a familiar wave of lethargy lulled her to sleep.

■ ■ ■

Ugh. Fuck. I'm late. I'm late for work, pregnant, and starving—what a combo!

Katelyn rushed through the doors of the hospital, adjusting the name tag swinging from her front scrub pocket. Her eyes scanned the lobby for the face she didn't want to see but knew she had to. She had anticipated waking up to a few missed calls or a least a text from Peter, but when she rolled over that morning, there was nothing. Radio silence, after she sent the most soul-baring two words of her life to a near stranger.

She continued looking until sure enough, there he stood several feet away from her, as relaxed as ever.

You can do this. Just go up to him! I'm sure there's a reasonable explanation for why he didn't write back. Maybe he didn't see it?

Katelyn took a deep breath and made her way over to Peter.

Baby daddy.

"Hey," she smiled faintly.

"Oh. Hey Katelyn. What's up?" Peter glanced up from his phone, leaving the reel of an OnlyFans model shaking her ass in plain sight.

Pig.

"So, did you get my message? I was surprised when I didn't—"

"Look, Katelyn. I don't know if this is some sort of joke or whatever, but your little stunt isn't going to work." His smoldering gaze burned into hers.

"Joke?! No, what? I'm really scared Peter, I don't—"

"Not to mention," he interrupted again, "if you really are, well, pregnant, how can you be so sure it's mine? I mean we only hooked up once, and that's as far as this will go." His hands motioned back and forth between them. "It wouldn't surprise me if you had a few regulars on rotation. Let's face it, that wasn't exactly your first rodeo."

Katelyn was speechless. She felt the tears rising again.

Keep it together.

She took a breath in through her nose, her eyes narrowing in on his once-gorgeous face.

"Yeah, well, you weren't exactly Leo DiCaprio," she said angrily. "Let's hope the next time I find myself in this *situation*, it's not the result of faking an orgasm with a guy who doesn't even have the decency to manscape. Go *fuck yourself.*"

Peter's face turned beet red. Katelyn's rant caught the attention of his classmates, as well as the attending physician. She only wished her words had been harsher, so he could feel a fraction of her pain. She blinked away her tears, abruptly turned and jogged to the elevator before he had a chance to retort. As the doors closed, Katelyn saw Peter's jaw clench as his superior approached.

Late, pregnant, starving, and heartbroken. All before 8 AM.

Katelyn swiped at her wet cheeks.

Fuck this. She took out her smartphone and messaged Tatum:

Katelyn: Techie. I need your help. Do you know how to
   hack into someone's email? Asking for a friend...
Tatum: Call me in five. I'm stepping out for a coffee.

This fucker had no problem disregarding my future so I'm going to mess with his.

15

WHITE COAT SYNDROME

Katelyn surveyed the waiting room, taking note of the people seated in the cold plastic chairs. Most were gloomily looking at their phones.

Are you waiting for someone? Are you getting an abortion? How do you know this is the right thing to do?

One woman was reading an expired issue of *People* magazine, her left knee bouncing up and down. A greasy-haired girl in an oversized grey hoodie was there alone. Her eyes scanned the room, too. She looked as depleted as Katelyn felt.

On one of the stark white walls a poster showed a woman prancing through a field, laughing with her stupid friends. Next to it, a cringy cartoon sloth dangled from a tree over the words, *"Hang in There."* One corner drooped away from the wall. Two plastic pamphlet holders contained stacks of brochures entitled, "How To Know Your Birth Control is Right For You" and "What It Means to Be HIV Positive." The only audible sound came from the wall clock—*tick-tick-tick*.

Like most girls, Katelyn had envisioned what it would be like to be pregnant. She'd chatted with her friends about wanting to be the "cute" pregnant lady. She'd only gain weight in her belly and wear empire waist dresses and colorful bikinis to emphasize the perfectly round bump. Her husband—someone she hadn't even met yet—would worship the ground she walked on and be just as excited as she was to become a parent.

Her mom would throw a baby shower at their house in Connecticut. Katelyn would post pictures of the kitschy gender reveal on social media. She's always wanted to start a family, which made her current situation feel like a cruel joke. Instead of basking in the joy of new motherhood, here she was in a dingy Planned Parenthood clinic in Midtown, biting her nails and wishing she could wake up from this awful nightmare.

Nat grabbed her hand as they approached the reception desk. "It's going to be fine. It'll be quick and then this will all be over."

Katelyn shook her head.

This will all be over for YOU. This will never be over for me.

"Are you sure you want to do this?" Nat asked, for the fifth time since getting in the Uber twenty minutes before.

"Yes, I'm sure," Katelyn mumbled. She couldn't deal with the prospect of any more contemplation. Her confrontation with Peter had sealed the deal.

"Okay. Women have been doing this since the dawn of time; you'll be fine." Nat squeezed her hand.

"I'd rather not talk about it if that's okay. This is a lot for me right now."

Nat stopped talking—her goal was to put Katelyn at ease, not upset her.

An overweight woman dressed in Snoopy scrubs looked up at the girls as she slid open the glass divider. "Do you have an appointment?"

Katelyn stuttered for a minute before eventually forming a sentence. "Hi. Yes, um. Katelyn Coppola."

The woman clicked buttons on her computer, then slid a clipboard across the small counter.

"Okay Miss Coppola. I'm going to need you to fill these forms out for me," she said briskly, before turning back to the screen. Clearly, she'd seen girls in Katelyn's state countless times before.

Katelyn looked at the form. It was the same one she'd given her own patients hundreds of times in the past, asking about medical history and preexisting conditions.

"Sit wherever you like and come back to me when it's done," the woman said without looking up. She slid the glass window shut again.

"Come on. Let's sit here." Nat guided Katelyn to two chairs near a young girl, no older than fifteen, who sat alone, scrolling through her Instagram.

Katelyn printed her name on the top of the page. She scribbled her date of birth and began mindlessly checking the boxes asking routine questions about her physical condition. There was more paperwork than she'd expected.

It's almost like they want me to have more time to think about it.

She knew that wasn't true, but still felt anxious when she skimmed over the "Understanding the Risks" section. She flipped to the last page, decided nothing printed in black and white would scare her out of doing this, dated the paper and signed her name. Then, after a heartbeat, she stood and made her way back to reception.

As Katelyn passed a poster that read, "Safe. Legal. Always Accessible," she felt ephemeral relief for the first time in weeks.

"Thank you, sweetie." The woman reached over to grab the clipboard. "And how are we going to be paying today?"

Katelyn had taken out a cash advance on two credit cards. Her very Christian parents also worked in health care. They'd surely question the procedure if the charge popped up at the end of the month. Insurance was out of the question, not that she was even sure it would be covered. She reached into her crossbody bag and pulled out a bundle of cash.

Nat pushed Katelyn's hand down. "Can we pay with a check?"

"Of course," the woman nodded.

"Great," Nat replied. She handed an envelope to the woman.

Katelyn poked Nat in the side. "Nat, it's too m—"

"Stop. Tatum and I know you're strapped for cash right now. We're taking care of this. You can pay us back when you can. You need to eat this month, don't you?" Nat asked as the woman handed her a receipt.

Katelyn blinked back tears. "Thank you. I—thanks."

The woman put the check in a drawer. "You can have a seat; we'll call you when we're ready."

The girls made their way back to the chairs. This time Katelyn grabbed Nat's hand. She thought about her life as a student, and the career she'd been working toward since the age of sixteen. She thought about her family, and what they would think if they ever found out, regardless of how much she wanted to confide in her mom. She thought about Peter.

Asshole.

Finally, she thought about the babies in the hospital. How they always soothed her, no matter how hard her day had been. She thought about their little hands, their chubby cheeks, and the pure joy they brought to those who cared for them. She felt guilty. How could the thing that gave her solace in a chaotic world be the very source of her misery?

I can't have a baby…can I?

Then someone called her name. She looked up and saw a blonde woman in pink scrubs, standing in the door to the hallway.

"I'll be right here when you're done, and we'll go to Shake Shack." Nat gave her a hug, and whispered, "Dawn of time."

Katelyn gave her a weak smile and walked toward the woman who led her down a long, stark corridor.

"The doctor will be with you in a few minutes for an examination and to go over some things pertaining to the procedure."

"Okay."

They turned into a room with an exam chair, and a framed photo showing a calm, blandly attractive woman smiling at her doctor.

Why the fuck are you so happy?

"Here's the gown. Fully undress and change into this, please."

The woman put a light blue medical gown on the stool in front of the exam table.

"The doctor will be in with you shortly," she repeated, shutting the door as she left.

Katelyn stripped off her oversized sweats. She stepped into the gown, tying it behind her back. The starchy paper crunched as she sat on the exam table. Katelyn had been in exam rooms like this countless times before, always comforting the anxious patients who sat across from her. Now she understood the tension and awkwardness they experienced.

She heard a knock at the door.

Breathe.

Seconds later, a young woman in a white lab coat walked in. "Hi, Katelyn. My name is Dr. Sawyer and I'm going to be performing your procedure today."

Katelyn swallowed against the lump forming in her throat. The doctor sat on the stool and rolled closer. "Before we do anything, I'm here to listen to you and answer all your questions. We're going to discuss every option and pursue the one that feels best for *you.*"

Katelyn started sobbing. "I'm sorry. I'm just really nervous and I never thought I'd be in this position."

The doctor nodded understandingly. "You don't have to be sorry. We're going to do this together."

Fucking Peter and his fucking toned arms.

She blamed him for putting her in this position, even though she knew it was as much her fault as his. Katelyn blamed him for denying his responsibility, then lashing out and insulting her in the process. She blamed herself for being stupid enough to have unprotected sex with a near-stranger when she knew better.

Angel-faced prick.

Then she thought about her mom. Katelyn knew she'd be distraught if she ever found out, but at that moment, all she wanted was for her mother to be there telling her everything would be okay.

■ ■ ■

Is it bad I've already masturbated twice today and it's not even noon?

Part of Nat felt guilty for sexting JP from the waiting room of Planned Parenthood. Here she was sitting with other women who were there for God-knows-what while she toyed with her new guy. All while her best friend was enduring one of the most violating and terrifying procedures of her life.

But she didn't feel guilty enough to stop. Nat had waited forever to find a guy she *actually liked*. Before JP, her friends had joked several times that she should make a trip to Riker's Island to find a "prison pen pal," AKA serial murderer, to fall in love with and marry.

But she wasn't that hopeless yet. So, a few months back she'd decided to give Hinge one more try. If that didn't work out, there was always Riker's.

She'd been seeing JP ever since, and while they weren't officially boyfriend and girlfriend, they were definitely *going on dates*. Not to be confused with "hooking up," "talking," or "exclusively dating but not boyfriend/girlfriend," and most definitely not "in a relationship." Things were going well.

Aside from the obvious physical benefits of having a man around, Nat liked how JP treated her. He was attentive but not overbearing, complimentary but not needy, and he possessed a certain confidence Nat attributed to his college athletic career. Plus, she couldn't keep her hands off the guy.

> God that's so hot. I'm so turned on just thinking about my mouth over every inch of you 😍😍

She looked around the somber room, wondering what she would do if she found out she was pregnant and the baby was JP's. She kind of thought he'd be supportive, financially and emotionally, and go along with whatever she decided to do. He was that kind of a guy.

As Nat floated away in a fantasy about JP as the potential father of her children, she caught the eye of a thirty-something man seated on the other side of the waiting room. He must have come in recently because she definitely would have remembered him. He was well-dressed in a Burberry suit and tie, his dark hair slicked back. He sat with his legs crossed exposing a Gucci patterned sock and sipped a large coffee. All while staring at Nat.

Well, well, well, what do we have here?

She met his gaze evenly before he shot her a coy but intentional smile. Nat blushed and bit her lip as her eyes darted back to her phone.

What kind of a perv flirts with strangers in an abortion clinic?

Surely, he had to be there with a woman. Why else would he be posted up in Planned Parenthood, sipping on a cappuccino? Maybe he had some bizarre fetish? She looked up again, and this time he let out a chuckle when he saw Nat's bashful expression.

Ew. He totally IS flirting with me!

Ping!

Nat looked down at her phone, surprised to see a message from Bill. She hadn't heard from him since Paris. She assumed her angry text was the reason. After deciding to delete his unread response, she'd made peace with likely pissing him off to the point of no return. She'd miss his bank account, but was actually relieved she didn't have to lie to her friends anymore, or JP. Nervously, she tapped the message.

Bill: Hello Natalie.

Ugh. I hate it when he calls me that.

> Bill: I need you for an event three Saturdays from
> now. Be sure to look youthful. I'd like for you
> to wear your hair up, minimal makeup will do.
> Marco will pick you up at 8.

Look youthful?! You're 72. Twenty-four IS youthful you creep.

Nat was immediately put off by both the tone of the message and its cryptic nature.

Ping!

Another text, but this was one from JP. Nat glanced at the clock on the wall to see how long it had been since Katelyn had gone in for her procedure. She could still feel the gaze from the pervy rich guy across the room, but smiled at the irony of three different men in three places all vying for her attention at the same time. That was a sensation she never thought she'd have, regardless if one of them had one foot in the grave and the other apparently had a thing for vulnerable women.

"Excuse me. You came in with Miss Coppola, didn't you?" Nat's train of thought crashed abruptly. She looked up to see the woman from reception standing in front of her.

"Oh, yes. Is she okay?" Nat asked, guilty for thinking about sex instead of her friend.

The woman smiled. "Yes, she's in the recovery room. She's asking for you. If you'll follow me, I'll take you to see her."

"Great, thank you." Nat stood, put her tote over her shoulder, and followed the woman. She gave the creepy guy a last look. He didn't hesitate to give her a full up-and-down.

Disgusting.

"She's going to be feeling a little crampy for the next few hours, and she should definitely rest for the remainder of the day," the woman instructed. "Make sure she takes it easy."

"I already have every Harry Potter queued up on her Netflix. She's not lifting a finger," Nat responded with a smile, feeling awkward about her rehearsed reply.

The woman opened the door to a pink and beige recovery room. "Push the button if you need anything."

Nat crept inside and saw Katelyn curled up under the starched white covers, her eyes shut tight. She felt a pang in her chest. She knew it would be a while before she had her bubbly, easygoing friend back. She took a deep breath and moved toward the cot.

"Hey Kate," she said softly. "How are you feeling?"

Katelyn's eyes fluttered open. "Nat," she said, in a scratchy voice.

Nat took a seat at the foot of the bed. "It's all over, Katelyn," she soothed, rubbing Katelyn's legs through the covers. "And before you say anything, I just want to tell you that I'm proud of you."

Katelyn rolled her eyes at Nat's remark.

"No, I'm serious. You just did something very brave—something you had to do. I'm proud of you for making the right decision, and I know this goes without saying—but I'm here for you no matter what."

Katelyn tried to sit up, whimpering for a second before managing to prop herself up on the pillow. "You don't know how much I needed to hear that right now," she said, motioning for Nat to come over and hug her.

Nat wrapped her arms around her friend. "Take as long as you need here. Tatum is meeting us at your place after work with food so we can all do nothing together."

"I got so lucky with you two," Katelyn mumbled.

Nat tilted her head to one side, surprised.

Katelyn was never one for sentiments.

"Speaking of getting lucky—I'm on a sex strike; it's caused me enough trouble so far," Katelyn announced, sliding back down onto the bed.

Nat smirked. "I'm holding you to that," she said, cuddling against Katelyn's legs.

16

POKER FACE

"Oh Natalie," Bill breathed as he drank in the visual of Nat's slender body draped in a canary-yellow strapless dress with a frothy tulle skirt that hinted at her shapely legs beneath. He lifted his Royal Courtesan cigar to his lips and braced his hands on the arms of the green velvet chair to lift himself up.

Here we go. Come on Gramps, you can do it.

Nat had to stop herself from cringing as he continued to struggle, finally straightening the jacket of his pale linen suit as he stood.

She had been looking forward to spending Tuesday evening alone when Bill texted her a few hours earlier, telling (not asking) her to be ready in 45 minutes for an impromptu "game night," whatever that was. As usual, his text had been cryptic.

Nat wasn't sure if that was intentional, or if he was just old and didn't understand texting. Regardless, she was somewhat relieved when they were greeted at the penthouse of the St. Regis Hotel for an ultra-high-stakes poker game worth no less than $500 million.

PRETTY GIRLS PLAYBOOK   163

When she walked into the spare, modern penthouse, Nat recognized two of the eight players seated at the round table, sipping scotch. One was a baseball legend —her dad was a huge fan. The other was a seasoned movie director known as one of Hollywood's most creative visionaries with an infamous reputation for paying male actors double what he paid their female counterparts.

The other five faces were much like Bill: older, clean cut, and clearly minted, as demonstrated by their Patek Phillippe watches and haphazard piles of cash. Some of the men wore designer suits, others were in pajama pants. All the female company, however, was dressed to the nines. Even the woman bartender was decked out in a vintage Valentino mini dress that hoisted her paid-for chest nearly to her chin, another piece of eye candy for the men to feast on as they carelessly gambled their millions.

The room was spectacular. The space spanned two floors encircled by window walls and a terrace offering a 360-degree view of the City. The poker table dominated the downstairs sitting room. Nat overheard one of the men mention that the African blackwood card table had just arrived from Dubai. He rounded out the comment with a vulgar joke about how the female help they'd hired for the evening had cost far more.

"Isn't it stunning?" The voice sounded like that of a young girl. Nat turned to see who was talking. "Drake Anderson designed this space for the evening; it's iconic."

Nat smiled at the girl who wore a bright pink floral midi dress that hugged her petite frame. She'd pulled her platinum hair into a sophisticated French twist.

"I'm sorry, I didn't even say hi! My name is Peyton."

"Natalie, but you can call me Nat. Are you from around here? I'm getting a little bit of an accent?"

"Oh gosh, no, I just moved here a few months ago when I got into Parsons to study design. I'm from Guthrie, Oklahoma."

"Well, welcome to the City."

"Peyton Anne," a booming voice interrupted their conversation. Nat looked up to see a man she didn't recognize, glaring at them with a proprietary eye.

"Oh shoot, Mr. Andrew hates when I socialize with the other girls too much. Says I'm too chatty. I'd better go. They'll be starting soon anyway. It was nice to meet you, Nat."

"You too, Peyton!" Nat couldn't help but feel bad for the girl. She watched as Peyton shuffled her way over to the old man, taking a seat on his lap.

Eighteen years old and all the way from the Breadbasket, just to sit on Mr. Andrew's lap. Girl, run.

■ ■ ■

After a three-hour game of poker and several near-misses from Bill's wandering hands, Nat stepped out to the terrace to get a little fresh air, seating herself in a comfortable plush deck chair. Her brief reprieve didn't last. After a couple of minutes, the French doors swung open, and Bill Hayes followed her outside. Without saying a word, he dragged a second chair in front of her and slithered into it, reaching out a papery hand to stroke her half-exposed leg.

"That was quite the game," Nat lied, forcing herself not to shrink from his touch. "How long have you been playing cards?"

Stupid question. Probably since before I was born.

"Oh, well, that right there was one of my best at Texas Hold 'Em." Bill's drawl sounded more prominent than usual. "And I've been playin' that since before you were born, little lady." His hand continued to stroke Nat's thigh.

Took the words right out of my head.

"Looks like I'm your lucky charm then!" Nat sat up and crossed her legs, trying to look chipper as she stared into Bill's wrinkled face. He took her hand in his and stared back.

"You certainly are," he agreed, a smile creeping across his face. Nat smiled back, unsure of how to subtly rebuff his advances. Bill leaned towards her, gently moving the piece of hair that framed her face behind her ear. He then moved his dry, thin lips onto hers.

Oh, come on, not again.

Nat locked her eyes on the Empire State Building in the background as Bill's tongue darted inside her mouth. She could hear the chatter from the other players on the terrace and felt overwhelmingly self-conscious. She knew they wouldn't dare approach a billionaire and his sugar baby in the midst of an intimate moment, but part of her hoped they would.

In the privacy of his car is one thing, but this is just humiliating.

Bill gently pulled away from Nat's kiss, his face lingering close to hers.

EW. What do I say what do I say?

"You even taste like a winner," she ventured, hoping he didn't see the deer-in-the-headlights look in her eyes.

"I feel like one too." Bill moved Nat's hand, which he was still holding, onto the bulge between his legs.

The only thing more cringe-worthy than that line is my hand on his actual crotch. I may have to fling myself off this balcony.

Wordlessly, he started to rub her hand over his boner.

An over-the-pants-hand-job? You've got to be kidding me.

Nat let out an uncomfortable giggle, but Bill kept going, pushing her hand to go faster. She looked up at the Empire State Building once more, fervently wishing she could teleport, as Bill's body quivered.

"Uhh, uhh," he groaned, shutting his eyes and stiffening, then slumping over the chair. She was speechless as he finally dropped her hand and took a deep breath.

"Definitely a winner," he croaked, still trying to catch his breath. "I'd better go clean myself up." He grinned and worked to heave himself off the chair. Without saying anything, Nat looked over her shoulder and locked eyes with Peyton, who shot her a genuine smile of solidarity.

Nat was still seated. When Bill finally managed to stand, her eyes locked on his stained linen pants, inches in front of her face.

What even is my life?!

Bill leaned over and kissed her on the forehead. "Looks like you're a winner, too." He flicked her a green plastic poker chip that Nat knew was worth $5,000. She sat motionless, still not having said a word.

"Oh, and Natalie," Bill said, as he made his way toward the doors, "next time, the stakes will be higher."

Nat sat upright on the chaise lounge, yanking at the sweetheart neckline of her gown to cover up more of her chest. She folded her arms and shivered; the nighttime breeze chilly on her bare skin. As she stared out at the New York City skyline, a lump rose in her throat. This was undoubtedly the most beautiful view of the City she had ever seen, but she had never felt so ugly.

All the way from Connecticut to jerk off a billionaire out on a balcony. Girl, run.

17

QUARTER LIFE CRISIS

Tatum stared at the new sequined red blazer dress hanging on the back of her bedroom door. She bought it a month before off Amazon when she was looking for the perfect 25th Birthday Bash look, on a budget. She had tried the Boutique de Bezoz dress on so many times, envisioning her most radiant self on the night of her birthday.

Now the dress reminded her of how much her life had changed. If you had asked her a few months ago, she would have said she'd be spending her 25th birthday with a loving boyfriend who'd planned a fun night filled with cheap liquor and embarrassing renditions of "Happy Birthday."

She thought 25 would be the year she went from a young-twenty-something to a grown woman, established in every aspect of her life. But the reality of being newly single made her feel like more of a mess than ever.

Not to mention that chaotic accidental hookup with Lola.

Since that night, Tatum couldn't stop thinking about Lola. While Lola had made it clear she had no intention of leaving her boyfriend, Tatum couldn't get their evening together out of her head. Lola's effortlessly sexy confidence made Tatum feel at ease. Then there was her tight, barely-there tank top. Her freshly glossed lips that looked wet.

Tatum's recent embrace of bi-curiousness had completely capsized the life she thought she had. The monogamous, straight, future Mrs. Blake Spencer was a shattered identity that seemed unfixable.

Needless to say, Lola wasn't invited to the party.

The party, Tate. Focus.

While Tatum had meticulously planned every element of her Emily Ratakowski-inspired look, Just Us Girls took care of the rest—the decorations, the guests, the club. She knew they'd be arriving soon to start the getting-ready ritual and kick off the night.

Pushing away her fantasies and trying to embrace the reality of her birthday, Tatum flung open the closet door and reached for the shoes stashed under mounds of professional attire. She rummaged around in a pile of cheap heels and old boots before slipping on her favorite pair of strappy black sandals. The rows of tiny metal studs in the leather reminded her of the Valentino pair she could nowhere near afford.

Tatum fastened the shoes and gently took the hanger with the sexy scarlet mini dress from the knob on the back of the door, holding the glimmering outfit against her figure. She admired her fresh cherry red pedicure in her favorite shoes and couldn't help but feel giddy. Even though she couldn't stop thinking about Lola or the fact that Blake wouldn't be there, Tatum was bubbling over with excitement.

I've been waiting a long time for tonight. I'm going to make 25 the best birthday yet! I deserve it.

She heard a knock at the front door, which had to be the girls. She kicked off her shoes and tossed the dress on the bed, quickly making her way to the entrance.

"Coming!" she yelled.

She flung open the door to see Nat and Katelyn in sloppy sweat-pant ensembles, each with a duffle bag in one hand and a bottle of Veuve Clicquot in the other.

"Happy birthday, *ma chérie!*" Nat yelled as she burst through the door with all her stuff.

Tatum grinned, taking the bottles of champagne. "Thank you. You guys are so sweet!"

"I don't know about you, but I say we pop some bubbly and get this party started!" Katelyn squealed, tossing her beat-up duffle on the floor.

Tatum laughed and gave her a tight hug. "How are you feeling?" she asked, unsure how the question would land. Katelyn hadn't quite been herself since the abortion, which wasn't a surprise. She put up a good front, but Tatum didn't want Katelyn to feel obligated to be anywhere—even on her birthday.

"I'm totally fine. Plus, tonight is about *your* sexy ass!" Katelyn reached for the pink plastic champagne flutes they'd set out for the party the day before.

"Okay, you're right. Let's pour ourselves a little *apéro* and then get started on hair and makeup." Nat dropped her bag on the floor and tied her wet hair in a high ponytail.

"I need help with *both*," Tatum admitted, handing Katelyn a bottle to pop the cork.

"Don't worry, I'll make you party-ready in no time," Nat reassured her.

"Everyone please gather around," Katelyn began, trying (and failing) to sound official. "I want to take a minute before everybody arrives and we all get a little crazy—or a *lot* crazy—to say, Happy Birthday to our Baywatch beauty Tatum Rose Kelley. Tatum, your boyfriend hired a Craig's List fire-crotch hooker to take a piss on him. It can only get better from here!" She raised both hands in the air and gave a double thumbs-up.

"Thank you so much for bringing that up," Tatum replied with a smile, her blue eyes shiny with affection.

Katelyn popped the champagne, prompting all of them to cheer. She quickly filled their glasses as a stream of bubbles spilled onto the floor. She lifted her drink high. "Now let's have a good time and make Tate's Twenty-Fifth a night to remember—or actually, a night we'll forget." The three girls clicked their plastic glasses and gulped the champagne.

Tatum put her drink back on the counter. "Okay. People are getting here around 9:30. We have two hours to do some damage control to *this*," she said, pointing to her silky blonde hair. Nat and Katelyn looked at each other and rolled their eyes. Even though Tatum had flung her blonde locks into a top knot, she already looked flawless. Tatum didn't need any preening; her look was always party-ready.

"Well, in that case, we better get started." Katelyn leaned down to pick up her the tote. They made their way to the bedroom, champagne in hand. Katelyn dropped the duffel again when she saw the sexy blazer dress on the bed.

"Oh My God," she gasped, reaching for the hanger. "Tatum. This is SO HOT."

Nat, who was unpacking her hot tools on the floor, looked up. "DAMN!" she screeched. "Did you invite that guy from work? The one you went on a date with? I think he'd appreciate seeing you in *that* little number. And out of it."

Tatum blushed. She looked at the dress, its sequins glittering in the natural light from the bedroom window. "I don't know if I'm going to wear it," she said shyly. "Don't the heels make it look slutty?"

"Absolutely *not*." Nat gestured for Tatum to take a seat on the floor where her curler was plugged in. "You only turn 25 once and that is just—" Nat mimed a chef's kiss.

"You're wearing it," Katelyn commanded, flinging the outfit back on Tatum's bed. She made her way to Nat's duffle. "What expensive thing do *you* have for me to wear, bougie bitch?" she asked cheerily.

Katelyn dumped the duffle on the bed and started going through Nat's arsenal of designer dresses, tops, and skirts. "Ooooh, I *love this*," she breathed, holding up the new leather jacket Nat had purchased with Bill's money a few days before.

"You can wear that. But be careful, it's Margiela," Nat warned, teasing the roots of Tatum's hair with a boar bristle brush.

"Yeah, I don't really care who made it. I just think it would look hot with the skirt I'm wearing."

Nat pursed her lips. "Just don't spill shit on it."

"*Deal*." Katelyn threw the jacket on the bed and began unzipping her own duffle, revealing a plethora of lacy tanks, tight skirts, eyeshadow palettes, and heeled sandals. She grabbed one of the palettes and rummaged around before locating her clear PVC makeup pouch. "I'm channeling Kim Kardashian Met Gala makeup vibes tonight," she announced, tucking her black hair behind her ears as she took a seat at Tatum's vanity.

"I love that for you." Tatum leaned back so Nat could curl the angled pieces of her hair framing her face.

"Oh, I almost forgot!" Nat propped the curler on the floor and picked up her champagne. "I made a getting ready playlist! Kate, connect my phone to the speaker."

Katelyn leaned over and grabbed Nat's phone from the floor next to the vanity.

"Who's Bill?" she asked, scrolling Nat's Spotify. "He keeps messaging you."

Nat's heart thumped.

Holy shit. I can't tell them now.

She swallowed her champagne and blurted out the first thing that came to mind.

"Bill? Oh, he's my dad's friend. He's in town for business and wanted to know some restaurant recommendations. He's probably just saying thanks." Trying to sound calm, she took another long sip of her bubbly.

"Ew, even so he could have not said 'Thanks for the delicious Tuesday.' What a fucking creep."

Uh, fucking creep is right.

The clapping beat of "Glamorous" by Fergie sounded from the speaker. Katelyn locked Nat's phone and put it face-down on the vanity next to her mess of makeup. Nat looked up at her friend and chuckled in agreement.

Crisis averted—for now.

"I could use a refill." Nat was desperate to calm her nerves. "Birthday girl, how about we step you up to a martini?" she asked, reaching for Tatum's plastic cup.

"Make it a double," Tatum winked.

Katelyn leaned into the mirror, intently focusing on the jet-black MAC liquid liner she was wielding. "I'm going to wait a few minutes. I can't do this even the slightest bit tipsy or I'll end up looking like Gene Simmons."

"Alright fine, but you just bought yourself a shot after you're done face-painting, Gene!" Nat cracked, walking to the kitchen.

■ ■ ■

"Alright, are you guys ready?" Tatum yelled over the loud music coming from the kitchen where Katelyn and Nat were waiting.

"Yes! Come out, come out!" Nat called excitedly, sipping her potent vodka soda through a straw, rather than ruin her flawless Chanel Palpitante red lipstick. She smoothed down her strapless white bodycon dress, an ode to the $6700 Givenchy Bill had bought for her. The real one was hanging in her closet; she couldn't bear to wear it to the downtown bars.

"You're killing us out here," Katelyn hollered, reaching for the ice tray, her tight midriff fully exposed in a miniscule bra top. Tatum's high heels clicked on the wooden floors as she made her way down the short hallway before emerging under the HAPPY BIRTHDAY balloons that hung in the kitchen doorway.

"What do you think?" she asked, giving a little twirl.

Nat and Katelyn stared. The blazer's plunging neckline revealed just the right amount of cleavage between Tatum's full breasts, and her tanned legs were toned and delicate. She looked nervously at the girls, the subtle smokey eye that Nat had done flawlessly complementing her glossy nude pout.

"Holy shit," Katelyn said, unable to look away. "No wonder Lola wanted to fuck you."

Tatum smiled, tucking her voluminous blonde curls behind one ear. "Really?"

"You look *incredible.*" Nat's voice was assured. "EmRata herself would be jealous." She pushed a vodka soda toward Tatum, who picked it up and took a long sip. Nat looked down at her phone. "JP and his roommates will be here in a few minutes. How about we all do a shot before they get here?"

Katelyn tipped back the remainder of her drink. "Perfect timing," she said, reaching for one of the handles of Tito's that were strategically placed amidst bottles of chasers, stacks of pink Solo cups, and a miscellaneous array of sweet and salty snacks.

"My head already hurts tomorrow. Nat, you're the worst bartender *ever.*" Tatum scrunched her face at her cocktail.

"Why do you think we're doing this on a Friday?" Katelyn said, filling three shot glasses with the thick, frozen vodka. "It's so we can have two full days to recover."

Nat took a deep breath. "Let's do it before I change my mind," she said, cracking open a lime La Croix. Katelyn pushed the shots glasses in front of the girls and raised her own.

Nat looked down at her shot, her stomach already rejecting it. "Only because I love you." She tipped her drink at Tatum before slinging it back.

The others followed suit, each slamming their shot glass on the counter.

"Ugh, that was so brutal. I have to sip a chaser before I can do that again," Tatum said, grabbing at Nat's cup.

Ping!

Katelyn looked around the kitchen. "Tate, I think that's you. There's definitely nobody texting me." She reached over the booze to grab Tatum's phone. She looked down at her friend's screen, her eyes widening.

"What?" Tatum asked, seeing Katelyn's reaction. "Was it me?" Katelyn looked at Nat, then at Tatum. "Ummm."

Tatum snatched the phone from Katelyn's hands and looked down. Her stomach dropped and the alcohol went straight to her head. *Blake.*

> Blake: Happy Birthday Gorgeous. I hope you have the best night because you deserve it. I think about you every second of every day. I love you and I always will.

Tatum's heart pounded. It was the first time she'd heard from Blake since their split. While she figured he'd moved on, it also made total sense if he'd been waiting until her birthday to give him an excuse to reach out. She put the phone down and immediately reached for the Tito's.

Nat glanced at the screen. "Tate, are you okay?"

Tatum downed another shot of vodka. "No," she replied in a quivering voice. "Who does he think he is? On my birthday? *Really?*" Tears started rolling down her face.

Nat poured three more shots. "It's not fair; he has no right to do this to you. *Especially* not tonight." She dabbed at Tatum's tears with a tissue. "Don't ruin your makeup. He's not worth it."

It was too late. Tatum's mascara was already smudged. "I can't believe it's my 25th birthday and he's *not here!*" she moaned. "I mean, here I am, single and all alone. I'm getting so *old* and I'm going to *die alone*. I work fifty hours a week, so I'll *never* meet anybody. I have no prospects. My life is so *depressing*." Tatum tried to wipe her wet face without completely destroying the look Nat had worked so hard on. "This is not how 25 is supposed to BE!"

Katelyn hugged her. "If you can't bag a husband with those tits then there's no hope for the rest of us. Eat this, you'll feel better. We don't need a Sienna 2.0 tonight," she said, her hand outstretched with a fist full of nut mix, conscious that her petite friend had already had a good amount to drink.

"I know and you guys are amazing. But the truth is, when I thought of myself at 25, I didn't see a single, insecure, broke girl— and that's exactly what I am," Tatum sniffled. "Oh, and did I mention I might be bi?" Katelyn's head jerked up. "Yup, after all that time with Blake, and now all of the sudden I can't stop thinking about girls. I don't know what the fuck is going on." Tatum threw her head in her hands.

"A blonde bombshell who also likes to eat pussy?! Tatum, you're a fucking gold mine." Katelyn tried to calm her down, suppressing the urge to grill her friend about the new sexual revelation.

Nat leaned in. "If you're bi, then that's awesome! Twice as many dating options. Tatum, you're exactly where you need to be."

Tatum picked up her shot and threw it back. "At least you don't have to worry about condoms," Katelyn muttered. Both girls giggled.

"Much better," Nat said, stroking Tatum's luscious hair. She couldn't help but shoot Katelyn a *we'll-revisit-this-later* look.

"Where's my phone?" Tatum suddenly asked, glancing around the mess of bottles and dirty shot glasses.

"You're not answering him, are you?" Katelyn looked concerned. "At least not tonight?"

Tatum grabbed her phone and got up from the stool. "No, we have people coming. I'm going to touch up my makeup," She turned and vanished down the hall.

Nat slammed her shot glass on the counter. "That was my last one," she said, making a face.

"Yep, you and Tila Tequila need to slow it down." Katelyn turned when she heard a knock at the door.

"Shit, that's JP," Nat said. "Go get her off her phone. Tell her we'll deal with the Blake thing tomorrow."

Katelyn nodded, following Tatum to her room at the end of the hall. Nat stood and adjusted the thin straps on her tight white dress, sucking in as hard as she could without seeming obvious. She flipped her hair and smiled wide as she opened the apartment door.

"Hey guys, come on in."

18

NEVER LEAVE A GOOD TIME TO HAVE A GOOD TIME

"Everyone SHUT UP! We're going to sing!" Nat teetered on her five-inch heels, towering over half the people around her. Her voice was drowned out by the thrum of guests talking and laughing, on top of the heavy hip hop playing in the background.

"WHERE'S TATUM?" she yelled at Katelyn, who was taking pictures with some of their friends against a balloon backdrop. Katelyn held up her hands and shrugged.

"Oh wait, found her!" Nat yelled. She caught a glimpse of Tatum, who was wandering toward the kitchen, her eyes unfocused. Nat looked down at the custom cake they'd ordered from a bakery on the Upper West Side that she'd found on TikTok.

Three tiers of strawberry cake smothered in thick, pale pink icing with pearl embellishments and delicate fondant flowers at the base of each tier. The whole concoction glowed with 25 long, sparkling candles and a glittery "25" topper. She motioned to JP to turn down the music.

"Haaaaappy Birthdayyyyy toooo youuu…" she started singing, bringing the cake out into the crowd.

She maneuvered her way toward Tatum, who stood mindlessly in the middle of the room. Tatum's hazy eyes lit up when she saw the glamourous cake, and her guests belted out the birthday anthem. Nat moved a few steps closer. Screens flashed on phones all around them as Tatum admired the towering confection.

"Make a wish," Nat said excitedly, putting the cake down on the table. Tatum took a deep breath and closed her eyes before blowing out the candles in one try.

"Smile!" Katelyn held up her phone and took a picture, capturing the moment.

Tatum flashed a big smile before addressing all the guests in the room. "Thank you so much you guys for coming. I don't really know what to say other than my life is a mess, but tonight, we're going to let loose and PARTAYYYY!" Even through her drunken haze, she radiated real joy.

"Take a shot!" one of the boys yelled from the back of the room, the rest of the crowd cheering in agreement.

"You don't have to tell *me* twice!" Tatum reached for the near-empty handle of vodka on the coffee table. She put the bottle to her mouth and chugged the rest of the liquor, feeling the flash of phones as her friends laughed and cheered.

Immediately, she felt sick.

I need a chaser.

She looked around, but there was no chaser in sight except the expensive, multi-tier cake. She reached out and grabbed, sticking her hand into one of the intricate floral designs. She ripped out a hunk of cake and buttercream, which she savagely shoved into her mouth.

Nat looked at Tatum in disbelief. "Okay, that's one way to do it," she said. "Tatum, are you okay?"

"Delicious," Tatum mumbled, crumbs spilling from her mouth.

"*Damn*, I like the 25-year-old you already!" Katelyn said, shoving her way in from the periphery and sliding her hand around Tatum's waist.

"I'm going to puke," Tatum whispered.

"I have to go to the bathroom. Come with me!" Katelyn sang out, loud enough for everyone to hear. She steered Tatum past their friends, beelining to the small bathroom. The music started blaring again as she shut the bathroom door, and Tatum flung herself over the toilet.

"Shit," Katelyn whispered, seeing for the first time how drunk her friend actually was. She ripped the hair tie off her wrist and tossed Tatum's elegant locks into a messy bun on the top of her head. Tatum looked up woefully, her eyes red and watery. "That last one really killed me," she mumbled, before projectile vomiting into the toilet.

"It's okay; get it out. Nobody outside knows. And anyway, it's your birthday. You can do whatever you want," Katelyn said reassuringly as she rubbed Tatum's back. The sight of Tatum puking immediately sobered her up.

There was a gentle knock. "Hey guys. It's me, can I get you anything?" The muffled sound of Nat's voice came through the door.

"My phone," Tatum gasped, "it's on the couch." She leaned over and retched again.

"Alright, I'll be right back!"

Tatum groaned as she laid her head on the toilet seat. "This is so embarrassing."

"No, you're fine. Nobody even knows." Katelyn got up and filled a plastic cup she found on the counter with tap water, handing it over to Tatum. "Drink that. It'll help."

Tatum lifted her head and reached for the cup, taking a baby sip before putting her head back down. "I can't," she mumbled hopelessly.

Nat opened the door the bathroom enough to shimmy through the small crack, locking the door behind her.

"Is everyone making fun of me?" Tatum asked.

"What? No. Everyone's too tipsy to even notice you're not out there, no offense," Nat replied, fixing her hair in the mirror. "I have your phone, by the way."

Tatum's head jerked up from the toilet. "Give it to me."

Katelyn crossed her arms suspiciously. "Why do you need your phone so bad?"

"No reason." Tatum ripped the phone from Nat's hands. She peered at the screen and started frantically typing.

"Who are you texting, honey?" Nat asked, looking at Katelyn, who shrugged her shoulders. "You were on the verge of death a second ago."

"Oh my God," Katelyn groaned, unable to hide her disappointment. "It's Blake, isn't it?"

Tatum looked up at her friends. "Whatever. It's my birthday. I can do what I want, remember?"

"Are you *kidding* me?" Nat shouted.

Tatum slumped against the wall. "No. We haven't spoken since the breakup, and we both have things to say. I know this is hard for you guys to believe, but I'm still in love with him. You can't just turn off five years of feelings."

"Tatum. He cheated on you. CH-EAT-TED, and then made a little home movie keepsake that should probably be up on FetLife. He doesn't care about you, and he doesn't respect you. No offense, but this kind of makes you look like an idiot." Nat didn't mean to sound so harsh, but she'd been drinking all night. And maybe she could force some sense into her friend if she was blunt.

But if Nat sounded harsh, Tatum was furious. "Are you fucking *kidding me*?" she spat. "You, of *all people*, are giving me *relationship advice*? Nat, you've never had anything *like* a real relationship, so how could *you* possibly know how I'm feeling?"

That hurt. Not only because Tatum's words held some truth, but because she knew how self-conscious Nat was about never having had a serious boyfriend.

"Don't listen to her," Katelyn said.

Nat bit her lower lip, trying hard not to say anything. She knew if she tried to defend herself, she'd just start crying.

Katelyn leaned toward Nat and whispered in her ear. "Look at her, she's so drunk."

"I'm not that drunk," Tatum slurred.

"Come on Tatum. It's your birthday and we've all been drinking. We want to have a good time! Maybe talk to Blake tomorrow. Nobody needs to get upset; let's just go back to the party." Katelyn reached out a hand to help her friend to her feet.

"I don't know how many brain cells you're missing, but I'm 25. Meaning, I'm an adult and I'll do what I want, and what I *want* is to talk to my boyfriend," Tatum snapped, struggling to stand.

Katelyn snorted. "Oh, he's your boyfriend now?"

"It's none of your business."

"Well, it's *going to be* my business when he cheats on you again and we have to come over here and hide all the knives, so you don't self-harm," Katelyn corrected, her eyes locked on Tatum's.

Tatum finally stood up tall, throwing back her shoulders. "Just like how it was MY business when you decided to fuck a stranger and kill your unborn child? Just like it was MY business when you couldn't even afford it and I paid for your abortion? You're *welcome*, by the way."

"Tatum, *shut up*!" Nat shouted.

Katelyn's eyes filled with tears. She started to shake, unable to speak.

Tatum's gaze shifted to Nat. "What, are we going to pretend like you're not sleeping around for money? We know what an intern makes and there's no *way* you can afford that wardrobe. Add that to you randomly being busy weekend nights. Come on Nat, it doesn't take a rocket scientist to figure out what *you've* been doing."

Nat's face flushed crimson. "You don't know what you're talking about."

"Whatever, why don't you go call Bill for more 'restaurant recommendations?'" Tatum mocked, doing air quotes. "I think he wants *sushi*."

"That was in seriously poor taste." Nat wrapped her arms around Katelyn, who had started to sob.

"*I hate you*," Katelyn whimpered, staring at Tatum who hadn't yet tried to apologize. She pulled away from Nat and unlocked the bathroom door, flinging it open. The sounds of the party filled the bathroom as Katelyn stormed out.

Nat turned back to Tatum. "Just because it's your birthday doesn't mean you get to be such a bitch," she said, still sweating from Tatum's accusations. She stomped out, leaving Tatum alone in the bathroom.

Nat eyed JP sitting on the couch and made her way over to him. "Hey, have you seen Katelyn?"

"Yeah, she just left. I was looking for you. Where have you been?" He stood and leaned in for a kiss. Nat dodged him, not in the mood to flirt.

"I have to find her," she muttered, turning back to the crowd. "I don't have time for this right now."

"Hey Nat!" Someone tapped her on the shoulder as she made her way to the doorway. It was Tatum's college friend, Holly. "Is Tatum, okay?" she asked. "I think she locked herself in her room and I heard crying. Maybe you could try talking to her?"

Nat closed her eyes, her head pounding from the booze and the heavy bass of the music. "I can't deal with this," she said, clenching her head in her hands. "EVERYBODY OUT. THE PARTY IS OVER!"

■ ■ ■

Tatum cracked her puffy eyes open as the light beamed in from her bedroom window. She lifted her head for a moment before immediately sinking back down.

Ugh.

The pounding was already setting in. She reached over to her night table and tried to gulp down the last of the lukewarm water she'd been sipping on the day before.

What the hell happened last night?

She had a sinking feeling the evening had taken a turn for the worse, but she couldn't pinpoint the details of what had happened. Sweating in the heat from the sunlight, she ripped off her down comforter and heard a groan she knew wasn't her own.

"Holy shit," she whispered. The familiar dark brown wisps of hair, strewn across the pillow beside her... It was Blake. The knot in Tatum's stomach got tighter. She examined his shirtless back and wondered how she could have forgotten her hysterical phone call to him. After her friends had left her in the bathroom. After their fight.

Shit. The fight. Flashbacks of her, Katelyn, and Nat in the bathroom now returned in pieces. She vaguely remembered a conversation about Blake.

Heart pounding, Tatum leaned over to the nightstand, ripped the phone from its charger and scrolled through her messages. She hoped there would be a message in Just Us Girls. They would never not text her after her birthday party to tell her they got home, but there was nothing.

She clicked opened her Instagram and was met with a flood of notifications telling her she'd been tagged in countless posts. Tatum paused a moment and took a breath before opening the first one, from none other than Lindsay Maddox. There she was, all of twelve hours before, pulling on a bottle of vodka and stuffing her face with cake to choke it down.

Tatum looked at the girl in the video and felt like she wanted to throw up. She heard Lindsay's shrill voice screaming in the background as she watched the replay of her drunk shenanigans, but she also saw Nat smiling happily. She looked at the time stamp: *11:16*

PM. So, the fight must have happened after that. Tatum frantically texted Just Us Girls:

> Tatum: Good morning!
> Tatum: So last night obviously was a little rough for me
> Tatum: I don't remember much, can one of you please call me?

She stopped typing when she heard the sheets rustling on the other side of the bed.

"Good morning beautiful," Blake croaked in his groggy morning voice, wrapping his arms around her body.

"Blake, what the hell happened last night?" She untangled herself from his grip and sat upright in bed. Her memory may have been foggy, but her voice was crisp and clear.

"You called me and told me you needed me to come over," he said, stretching his arms out with a yawn. "You said you and the girls had a huge fight and you didn't want to be alone."

"Did I say what the fight was about?"

Blake chuckled. "I don't know Tate, something about Nat being a secret prostitute and Katelyn a child murderer. You were on one, that's for sure."

Tatum's mouth went totally dry.

Oh my God.

She looked at her phone once more. Still nothing from either of the girls. She shot up from the bed and started pacing the room, forgetting all about the hammering pain in her head.

"This isn't funny. I think I really screwed things up." She grabbed the phone from the sheets and dialed Katelyn's number.

"Pick up, pick up!" she muttered, as the line went straight to voicemail. "Damn it."

Blake propped his pillows against the headboard and took his phone from the nightstand. "This video of you chasing the vodka with cake is pretty funny," he commented with a laugh.

"Blake, *what the hell?* Can't you see I'm stressing out here? I think I ruined both of my most important friendships last night. Can you not talk about the cake? I know I may have drunkenly asked you to come over, but that doesn't mean we don't have a lot to talk about. I don't even know if I forgive you, and I *definitely* don't trust you."

"You trusted me enough to try and fuck me last night," he said, still scrolling through his phone.

"What?"

"Oh, come on. You and I both know the cake wasn't the only thing you wanted to take down. I mean you passed out five minutes after I got here, so our reunion was less-than-climactic. But still, it was nice to wake up next to you again. I missed it."

The knot in her stomach tightened again as she swung open her closet and started tossing clothes on the ground.

Did he try and have sex with me? I was so drunk; I don't even remember inviting him over!

Her face turned red as she grabbed a black hoodie and pulled it on over the T-shirt she was wearing. Then she bent and slid on a pair of Lululemon track shorts, tying her hair in a high ponytail, her wilted curls flopping to one side. "I'm going to Nat's," she declared, walking into the small hallway that led to the living room.

"Do you want me to go with you?" Blake yelled from his post on the bed, still not looking up.

"No, I want you to clean up my trashed apartment." She made her way past scattered empty bottles, kicking a plastic Solo cup across her sticky floor before finally making her way to the door. She took a deep breath.

"I love you," Blake yelled. She slammed the door without a reply.

Tatum was anxiously standing in front of the elevator when she felt her phone buzz. She looked down, half-relieved and half-scared when she saw a message from Nat:

Nat: I'm on my way to my parent's house. I need some time; we can talk when I get back?

She needs some time? Holy shit, it's that bad?

Tatum's fingers couldn't move fast enough:

Tatum: Ok. I really need to talk to you when you get back. Enjoy Connecticut. I'm sorry.

She hit Send and took a seat on the cold pleather chair by the elevator.

Tatum, what the hell did you do?

19

THERE'S SOMETHING ABOUT SUBURBIA

Nat looked out the window as the Metro-North train quietly hummed through the little shoreline stations. Even though she lived only a few hours away by train, she hadn't been back to her hometown since Christmas. Nat hadn't even considered an impromptu trip home until she'd sat on her apartment bed the night before, drunk and crying. That's when she realized she was in desperate need of her mother's TLC and a steaming plate of home-cooked food. She'd packed her duffle bag and taken the first train out of Grand Central back to Connecticut that morning.

She was still processing the previous night's events, namely the blowout argument that had derailed the entire evening before it even began.

How did Tatum figure out I was being shady with money? Why didn't she say something earlier if she suspected something? Prostitution, really?

Despite Tatum's cruel words, deep down Nat felt like her friend's drunk tantrum had given her the reality check she needed, forcing her to ask some hard questions. Sienna's alcoholic meltdown in Paris got her fired, but she promptly checked into an outlandishly expensive rehab facility in Vermont. Then the firm brought in yet another bitchy temp manager. She was every bit as demanding as Sienna, constantly working Nat and Poppy to the bone in preparation for New York Fashion Week.

Most of Nat's days brimmed with appointments, order forms, and fittings, but she was still treated like a replaceable, ungrateful intern. Between grueling days at Marcheline that ended with a fast-food burger at 10 PM, and witnessing Sienna's depressing fate after years in the industry, Nat had started questioning her future in fashion.

With her career up against a dead end, Nat started to look at other parts of her life like JP. She didn't know what their future would be like, or even if there would *be* a future, but she was sure about one thing—she loved spending time with him.

In a perfect world, they'd be boyfriend and girlfriend, and he'd meet her family as her plus one at Margot's wedding in six weeks. But, in her actual messy world, not only did she have no idea what JP wanted out of their relationship, she also felt herself pulling away in fear. Plus, she still had to deal with the other complication in her life—Bill.

The conductor's voice crackled over the PA system. "Next stop is Wexler." Nat straightened and unplugged her phone from the outlet under the seat. She unlocked the device to send a text to her mom:

Nat: Hi Mommy. You're picking me up from the train
    station, right?

She gathered her bags and heard a ping as she made her way to the door at the end of the aisle.

Mom: I even have a coffee waiting for you :)

Nat smiled, relieved at the thought of all of the (s)mothering she'd be getting for the next day and a half. The train slowed, then rolled to a stop in front of the old-fashioned platform with a quaint sign reading "Wexler" in a simple black lettering.

Nat stepped out, the warm summer breeze caressing her shoulders. She took a deep breath and enjoyed a moment of country quiet, something she'd nearly forgotten. She made her way down the steps into the parking lot, and towards her mom's black Audi, her Vera Bradley duffle hoisted over her shoulder.

"Natalie!" her mom shouted as she stepped out from the driver's seat, her dark brown coiffe blowing in the wind. "I'm so glad you're home!" She wrapped her arms tightly around Nat.

"Me, too." Nat hugged her mom back, instantly soothed by the nostalgic Clinique scent she'd been wearing since Nat was a child.

"Come on. Your dad is waiting to see you." Her mother released Nat and got back behind the wheel. "Almond milk iced caramel macchiato," she said with a smile, handing an icy Starbucks cup to Nat in the passenger seat. Nat took the drink and popped in the green straw.

"Thank you. This is just what I need." She took a long sip of the creamy goodness.

Nat cracked the window of her mother's immaculate car and scanned the scenery as it passed. The trip already felt therapeutic.

"Okay," her mom started. "Tell me what's been going on. I want to hear all about the girls and that new guy you've been seeing."

"Mom. I literally just got in the car; can we talk later? I'm trying to relax for a minute." Nat sounded a more aggressive than she'd intended. "I mean, we'll chat about me later. Why don't you tell me about everything here? How's grandma doing?"

Nat's mother rolled her eyes, a habit she'd passed on to her daughter. "She's good. She misses you—you know Grandma, she always has something to say. The other day she was complaining because she's 'sick and tired of being the only young soul in the place.'"

Nat laughed at the thought of her dad's mom, the fiery white-haired woman who had taken charge of her assisted living complex the day after moving in. "I'm going to visit her tomorrow," she decided.

"Other than that, not many changes around here these days." Nat could feel her mom's eyes as she scrolled her Instagram feed with one hand.

"You're such a beautiful girl, Nat," she said, reaching over to stroke her daughter's head. "I just wish you would leave your hair alone. You don't need that blonde crap in it; your natural color is much more flattering."

"Mom *please*."

She'd figured her mom would have something to say about her fresh balayage, and she didn't need to hear it. These were the highlights she'd pleasured an old man to afford, after staring at pictures of 90s-era Jennifer Aniston for months.

"I'm just saying," her mom continued, "I don't know why you need to mess with yourself. Why don't you just get a new lipstick if you want to switch up your look?"

"Because highlights are what young women do, okay? This isn't the Fifties when you could get away with un-plucked eyebrows, and a little black eyeliner made you the homecoming queen."

Nat sighed, thinking to herself how Katelyn would've laughed if she'd heard that.

"Well, I wouldn't know what they did in the Fifties because I wasn't alive." Her mom shot her a wry smile.

Nat couldn't help but laugh. "That's right, you were an '80s babe." She chewed the straw poking out of her drink.

"You would not *believe* the nightmare the caterer has been for your sister's wedding." Her mother sipped from the lipstick-stained lid of her own Starbucks cup.

Nat lit up. She loved talking about her sister's upcoming big event. Especially with her mom, since she cared about the wedding as much as, if not more, than Margot herself. Her mom could talk about caterers, florists, and seamstresses all day, which was a far cry from the bored expressions Nat got when she brought up the wedding with her friends and coworkers in the City.

"I swear this wedding is making me go gray," her mom said dramatically, running her fingers through her hair. Nat listened as her mom went on about every detail of the catering fiasco, which wasn't a fiasco at all—only their reluctance to serve cocktails thirty minutes before the main course.

Champagne problems.

Instead of resting on the wheel, her mother's hands moved with exaggerated animation. She talked a mile a minute, only pausing for the occasional swig of her coffee. Nat hadn't seen her this excited… well, ever. When Nat was growing up, her mother had maintained parenthood was her *joie de vivre*, always telling Nat and her sister she was "born to be a mom."

Something about watching her relate the caterer drama, however, made Nat wonder if that had been the truth. For a split second, she wondered who her mom had been at her age.

Oh wait. She was married.

By thirty, she had two kids and a commitment to full-time motherhood until she was sixty.

Is that the kind of wife JP wants?

Nat knew her parents had a decent marriage, and her mom had a carefree life filled with Pilates classes and $30 salads with her book club, but...

Three decades of playdates and soccer games, only to obsess about caterers and cocktails? That's your joie de vivre?

■ ■ ■

Nat lay cuddled up on the leather sectional in the living room with reruns of "Law & Order" playing on the large flatscreen. She heard her dad's heavy breathing as he made his way over to the couch. Nat scrunched her legs to make room for him.

"How are you honey?" he asked, flopping into the cushion close to her.

Nat looked up from her phone and tossed it on the coffee table. "You know, just trying to get by."

Her dad laughed and leaned back. "You're 24; these are the fun years! How are you doing with money? Do you need any help?"

Nat could tell he was being sincere.

Um yeah. How much can you give me?

"No, I'm good for now. Luckily work pays me overtime, which is unusual for an internship," Nat lied. She knew her parents could always give her money if she really needed it. But the thought of taking a handout after they'd supported her for 22 years and paid for private college made her uncomfortable.

"I was hoping you'd say that. Your sister is draining me dry with this wedding. And did your mother tell you she has her eyes on a kitchen remodel?" Her father's big hands pinched the bridge of his nose under his cloudy glasses. "How's work? You happy there?"

Nat wasn't sure if she should lie this time since her happiness was the only thing her parents seemed to care about. "I mean, it's a lot. Honestly, Dad, I've considered looking for something else," she mumbled, afraid her response would disappoint him.

"Nat, you're a smart girl and you can do anything you put your mind to. I've always told you that." He stretched his hand out and put it on her leg. "You need to be somewhere they really value you, and where they have a 401K match program. That's also important."

Nat smiled. "Thanks Dad, I'll keep retirement in mind."

"I'm throwing a burger on the grill, you want one?"

"Yes please, with cheese."

"Okay, sweetheart." He leaned over and kissed her forehead before he got up.

Nat watched as her dad went to the patio door to fire up the grill—one of the simple pleasures of fatherhood. She felt guilt ridden. If her parents found out what she was really doing for money, selling her time like a commodity, they might have preferred she donate her eggs after all. Nat's phone buzzed from the coffee table.

Please, please, don't be Bill.

She looked down to find a message from Katelyn:

Katelyn: I should've come home with you…

Nat: I wish you did. It's so relaxing. How are you feeling?

Katelyn: I don't know, depressed. As if I wasn't dealing with enough emotions before, I just can't believe she came at me like that

Nat cringed at the thought of Tatum's cruel words that had cut Katelyn so deep.

"Dad?" she called out, still horizontal on the couch. "I'm good on the burger for now. I forgot I made plans to go see Grandma." She got to her feet. "I'm taking the Jeep. I'll be back later."

■ ■ ■

Nat ignored the "Residents Only" parking sign in front of the three spots near the nursing home entrance and slipped the oversized Jeep between the narrow lines. She grabbed a farmer's market bouquet of peonies from the messy passenger seat and hopped out. As she walked through the automatic lobby doors, she felt elderly men and women staring at her. She figured they were probably judging her ensemble: a pair of sky-high espadrilles and a bright red floral sundress—so she sucked in her stomach and puffed out her chest to give them a show.

She approached the desk and cleared her throat. "Hello. I'm looking for Claire Reardon."

"Would you look at my *beautiful grandbaby?* Welcome to God's waiting room!"

Her grandmother's greeting echoed in the spacious lobby as she shuffled toward Nat.

The woman behind the desk laughed. "Claire, behave yourself. You wouldn't want the other residents getting upset now, would you?"

"Those old coots can't hear me anyway."

Nat leaned down to hug her diminutive grandmother. "Hi, Grandma. I missed you so much!"

"I missed you too, baby girl." The older woman's frail hands held onto her. "Let's go talk in the game room. Bingo should have ended by now." She took Nat's hand and led the way.

The two sat on one of the dark green couches in the large room, a pot of burnt coffee and a box of Entenmann's coffeecake forgotten on the table in front of them. Nat's grandma had her room of course, where they would usually go for a chat, but since her stroke six months prior, walking up the stairs had become more difficult. These days, she preferred the ground floor.

"How are you. Do you like it here?" Nat put down the bouquet of peonies and took her grandmother's hand.

"It's not the Taj Mahal, but my nurse is a doll and I have my group of friends," her grandmother said. "But you didn't come here to talk about who's fighting over crossword puzzles. Tell me about *you* and your fabulous life in New York City!"

Nat could tell her grandma was excited to talk about her. Sometimes it seemed she lived vicariously through her granddaughter's carefree lifestyle.

"It's good," Nat said. Her voice sounded weirdly high-pitched.

Her grandma didn't skip a beat. "Okay, what's going on? Tell me everything. I knew something was bothering you when you sent me that text message about *the one*."

"Ugh. I don't know." Nat wasn't sure where to begin. "Nobody said adulting would be this complicated."

Her grandmother's eyes looked pained.

"It's everything. Like last night we threw Tatum a 25th birthday party. She drank a lot and said some pretty hurtful things to me, and especially to Katelyn."

"Oh honey, you know alcohol makes you say things you'd never dream of saying sober." Her grandma patted her hand. "Why do you think I gave my first husband an ultimatum? I couldn't handle his booze talk anymore."

"I mean, we've been friends our whole lives. How could she be okay with being so cruel?"

"Sweetie, I doubt she's 'okay' with it. Have you spoken to her? Given her a chance to explain herself?"

Nat hated that her grandma was defending Tatum, but she also knew she needed to hear the voice of reason.

"No."

"Natalie, life is too short to lose the people you love. Look at me. Do you know what I would give to have one more night on the town with my best friend Joan? The relationships you have with your girlfriends are all you have to keep you sane. Talk to her."

Nat knew she was right, but she wasn't quite ready to admit it.

Sensing her reluctance, her grandmother changed the subject. "Okay, now tell me about the boy!"

"Which one?" Nat quipped.

"That's what I like to hear," her grandma laughed.

"It's complicated. Did you ever do something you felt really guilty about, but weren't sure how to get it under control?"

Her grandma lowered her voice and leaned in. "Honey, I married a man I met at Woodstock after twelve hours. I'm assuming this is about the multiple boyfriend dilemma?"

Nat smiled. "Well, yeah, you could say that."

"I don't care how many beaus you have or how many 'hookup pals' or whatever your generation calls them, so long as they're treating you right. You can do whatever you want, but the second they start taking advantage, it's time to rethink your situation. I *mean it.*"

She reached for the box of cake and cut a slice. "Do not let any man make you feel less than the goddess you are Natalie!"

"You're right. I lost sight of that." Nat watched as her grandma served the cake, reaching for the last two plastic forks by the coffee pot.

"*Damn right* I'm right. You're young, beautiful, talented, smart, and if a man isn't fawning all over you—*drop him.* Now let's finish this cake and blame it on Betsey; she let me win in Scrabble yesterday."

Nat took a fork, giggled, and shook her head. "Never trust a Betsey!"

■ ■ ■

"Come *on!*" Nat shouted in the privacy of the car when she saw the main road closed for construction. She swerved the black Jeep Wrangler toward the detour sign and took an unfamiliar gravel road. She turned down the John Mayer on her stereo. She vaguely recognized this place. When the dust settled and she got back on pavement, Nat immediately knew where she was: the road to her old high school.

She drove by the massive brick building slowly, thinking back to her years there that seemed a lifetime ago. There were the stadium lights by the football field, the same ones that had shined on her red and gold cheer uniform on Friday nights. There was the parking lot where she'd illegally carpooled with her friends and made out with boys in the back seat of her car. She thought about Katelyn and Tatum, and how the three of them had been as inseparable back then as they were now. Then she thought about the fight. The Tatum she'd known in high school would never have said those things.

Shit.

Out of the corner of her eye, Nat noticed the yellow gas light on the dash. She knew there was a Seven Eleven on the road ahead, after the stoplight. She was stopped at the light when she heard whistling from the car next to her.

"Hey baby, where you going?"

Nat looked to her right to see three high school boys in letterman jackets hanging out the windows of a beat-up Acura.

"What do you say you hop in, and we'll take you for the ride of your life!" The boys in the backseat roared with laughter.

Oh boys. One day. One day you will cringe at this version of yourselves and hope that your daughter never crosses a pack like you.

She threw them an amused smile then turned up the stereo before stepping on the gas as the light turned green.

"Aww come on," one of the voices shouted behind her. She couldn't help but smile. Her mom was right. No matter how much time went by, nothing about Nat's hometown seemed to change— except for her.

20

ICED

Katelyn jumped when the black buzzer on her table vibrated. "I'll try and bring everything; you stay here," she told Nat. Moments later she returned, struggling to balance two trays filled with their Panera Bread favorites.

Nat scooted out of the booth, taking one of the trays. "Wouldn't want you to spill on that outfit of yours," she joked, nodding at Katelyn's vibrant scrubs.

"Broccoli cheddar soup would be the least offensive fluid on them today."

"Foul," Nat replied, sliding back into the tight booth. "So," she said, sipping on her fountain Diet Coke. "Have you talked to her?"

Katelyn tore her bread and focused her big blue eyes on Nat's. "No."

"Katelyn, I know she was a huge bitch and said things, but I think you would feel better if you spoke with her about it. I mean, it's been almost two weeks." She stirred a teaspoon of dressing into the spring mix on her plate.

"Nat, I understand she apologized to you a million times and you forgave her, but she said things to me that I don't know if I can get over. Every time I consider going to talk to her, I think about the abortion, and I can't handle it."

"Kate, she was drunk."

"I don't care." Nat could see that Katelyn was getting upset. "I know you hate confrontation, but she called you a prostitute and you got over *that* pretty quick." Katelyn spooned the chunky soup from her bread bowl.

Nat knew it was time to tell Katelyn the truth about being a sugar baby. Her Connecticut retreat had ended with a late-night phone call to Tatum explaining how she wasn't *exactly* a prostitute, but she *had* been spending time with a 72-year-old for cash. Tatum had been surprisingly casual about it. Nat wasn't sure if that was because Tatum was trying to get back in her good graces, or if she genuinely didn't care, but it seemed like Tatum's only gripe was that she hadn't known sooner.

Nat watched Katelyn slurping down her Dr. Pepper. "Okay, I have to tell you something." She tried not to sound too serious.

Katelyn stopped slurping. "What?"

"You have to promise you won't judge me."

"I won't."

"I mean really, this might sound kinda bad."

"Nat, you're scaring me. What the hell *is* it?"

Nat took a deep breath and a final sip of her diet soda. "So, obviously you remember Tatum calling me a prostitute."

"Holy shit, are you a prostitute?" Katelyn cut her off without lowering her voice, causing some of the other people in the dining room to glance over.

"No!" Nat yelled defensively. "But I haven't been exactly truthful about…you know…the money."

"What money?"

She's really going to make me spell it out for her, isn't she?

"Everything. The designer clothes, the shady Saturday nights when I'm not around…"

"Nat, what are you saying?"

"I have a sugar daddy," Nat blurted out.

Katelyn dropped her spoon and her jaw fell open.

"His name is Bill. He's 72 and he's loaded. He's not like my boyfriend or anything, but I spend time with him and he pays me— sometimes in cash, sometimes in clothes." Nat knew full well the table behind her was savoring her bombshell.

Katelyn just blinked.

"Can you say something please?" Nat pleaded.

"Are you fucking with me?" Katelyn finally said, with a hint of amusement.

"Honestly, I kind of wish I was."

Katelyn burst into roaring laughter, doubled over the table in a matter of seconds. Nat, flooded with relief, couldn't help but laugh with her.

"Wait," Katelyn gasped, as streams of tears rolled down her face, "you're telling me…" She could barely finish her thought. "That you've been spending time with an old man for *cash?*"

Nat took a breath. "Basically."

Katelyn took a sip from the small cup of water next to her soup, the water spilling through her lips moments later as she once more broke out laughing. "Woo. Okay." She giggled. "Why didn't you *tell me?*"

"I don't know. I was so embarrassed, and I didn't know how

you guys would react. I mean in the beginning, I meant to tell you, but then once it all started happening, telling you guys would've made it somehow more real. Plus, it's not like I see him all the time. It's only been a few times. But I *am* supposed to go with him to some event on Saturday."

"I have so many questions." Katelyn tore off another piece of her bread bowl. "Like have you kissed him?" She leaned in. "You haven't seen it, have you?" Nat threw her head back to hide her smile. "Oh my God, what does it look like?"

"Katelyn can we not? I'm eating."

"Like a little shriveled baby carrot, I bet. Does it still work at that age?"

Nat choked down the salad she'd just forked into her mouth. "KATELYN!" she shouted, before lowering her voice. "A little too well. They take pills to make it work, I think. Honestly, I don't want to think about it." Nat glanced at the sad breadstick in front of her.

"Wait," Katelyn said, looking directly at Nat. "Does JP know?"

"*Hell* no," Nat replied, trying to mask her guilt. "I can't tell him. We're not even official. How do you think he would feel if he found out I was blowing him off to spend time with Gramps?"

"As long as you keep blowing him…" Katelyn winked at Nat.

"What is *wrong* with you?" Nat laughed. "JP doesn't know. Only you and Tatum know." Katelyn visibly cringed at the mention of Tatum's name.

"Well, your secret is safe with me," she declared after a brief pause. "Wait, so how much money are we talking?"

Nat looked up from her salad with a mischievous smile.

■ ■ ■

Nat lit her Anthropologie candle and sipped the strong, lightly creamed coffee from her favorite mug as she admired the dozen multicolored tulips JP had brought over the day before. He said he saw the flowers on his way home from work and they reminded him of her, which made her smile. She took a seat on her uncomfortable loveseat and looked outside as the rain splashed the buildings outside.

Julia had gone on some godforsaken camping trip and this was one of the first Saturdays Nat had the place to herself. Once JP had left that morning after making her breakfast in bed, she'd taken the opportunity to deep clean the apartment and enjoy some peace and quiet, *sans* squid smell, before the girls got there.

She looked up when she heard someone rattling the doorknob. "It's me, I'm using the spare!" Tatum's voice came through the thin door. Nat adjusted the oversized biography of Coco Chanel on the low glass coffee table and stood up to greet her friend.

Tatum threw open the door, soaked from the downpour outside. "Do you have a sweatshirt? I think I have hypothermia." She propped her umbrella up by the door, creating a small puddle on the doormat.

"Want some coffee?" Nat asked, as she tossed Tatum a towel and an XL Villanova hoodie. Tatum had already stripped down to her bra and leggings. Nat went over to the mini espresso machine and freshly ground beans on the kitchen counter.

"Vanilla please," Tatum replied, toweling her hair. "Nat, I'm so nervous about how this is gonna go." She took the steaming mug from Nat's outstretched hand. "I mean, it's been three weeks and she won't respond to me at all."

Nat took a sip from her cup. "I mean, she won't have a choice.

I'm sick of this and I know she is too. Katelyn is stubborn and we know that, but I'm literally not letting anyone leave until this little tiff is over. I feel like I'm splitting my time between divorced parents and I'm over it." She popped a handful of Marcona almonds in her mouth from the delicate ceramic bowl atop the low coffee table.

Nat heard her phone buzz and looked down to a message from Katelyn. "Okay, she's here," she said, putting her cup on a coaster and going to the door.

Tatum froze. "I'm going to stay here so she can't see me until you let her in."

Nat nodded and slid open the lock.

"Literally raining so hard outside!" Katelyn burst through the door in her oversized windbreaker, struggling to rip off her Hunter boots. "I can't *wait* to watch movies all day."

Nat shot a quick look at Tatum. "Before movies, we have some business to take care of."

Katelyn's eyes followed Nat's, landing on a terrified Tatum standing in the living room.

"Nope, not doing this." Katelyn reached for the boots she'd just taken off.

"Katelyn, please. I have to talk to you," Tatum pleaded, slowly stepping toward the doorway.

"Well, I don't want to talk to *you!* I'm done with you, Tatum!" Katelyn yelled, her cheeks hot.

"Listen!" Nat chimed in. "I know this is hard for you Katelyn but be real. Tate is your best friend and she's here to apologize. Can you let her speak for a second?"

Katelyn's look shot daggers at Nat. "She *was* my best friend.

Before she degraded me about the most traumatizing event in my life."

Tatum moved closer. "I'm so sorry! I was shitfaced! And I know that's not an excuse, but you *know* I would never say anything that cruel to you!" Her voice cracked.

Katelyn stared at Tatum, her arms crossed.

"I am *so sorry*. I wish I could take it all back. I *don't* judge you for the decision you made, and I hate myself for making you think that I do." Tatum started to cry. "I-I-I'm *so so sorry*, Katelyn. *Please* forgive me."

"You really hurt me," she said quietly.

Tatum walked over to her and wrapped her arms around Katelyn's wet body. "I know, and I'll never do it again."

Nat had made her way to the kitchen, still in earshot of her friends making up.

"Well, if it's any consolation, I gave Bill an over-the-pants hand job at poker night," Nat called out over her shoulder, taking a sip of her coffee.

"Okay. First of all, that is so gross. I need details," Katelyn said, Tatum's arms still wrapped around her. "And second of all, Tate I love you but if you ever come at me like that again, that'll be it."

With that, she returned the hug, finally giving her friend the absolution she needed.

"Aw, is this finally a *truce*?" Nat squealed as she darted over to her friends and threw her arms around them both. "UGH! I missed us!" She squeezed them hard. "Can we *please* move this conflab to the couch so we can finally catch up on all of our shit?"

The three girls untangled from one another.

"Nat," Katelyn said, removing her sopping windbreaker to

reveal a baseball hat that shadowed her usually bright eyes. "I need coffee."

"Already poured; it's on the counter." Nat snuggled up once more on her loveseat, wrapped in her favorite TJ Maxx fleece blanket. Katelyn went to the kitchen, grabbed the mug, and returned to the living room.

"So, what happened to you that night?" Katelyn asked. "You like kind of died."

"I *know.*" Tatum threw her head back with a groan. "I drank *way* too much. You guys are going to die though, for real." She covered her face with her hands.

"What?" Nat asked.

"So, obviously I don't remember much," Tatum said, peeking through her fingers. "But I knew it was a rough night when I woke up and saw you-know-who lying next to me."

"Blake?" Katelyn asked, sitting on the rug in front of the coffee table. "You woke up next to *Blake?"*

Tatum blushed furiously. "Um, maybe?" Her voice went up an octave.

"What does that mean? Have you guys been talking?" asked Nat calmly. She shook her head at Katelyn, signaling her not to be too harsh. Disapproval was written all over her face.

Tatum picked at a loose thread on the blanket. "We've been talking, trying to work things out."

As usual, Katelyn went straight to the point. "Have you had sex?"

"Nonstop."

Nat ran her fingers through her hair. "You're so screwed. You're getting back together, aren't you?"

"I don't know. I mean, I love him. I never stopped loving him."

"As long as you're happy," Katlyn sighed, in a surprisingly supportive tone. "And while you're at it get an extra dicking in for me—I'm still abstinent."

Her friends laughed.

"It's only a matter of time," Nat reassured her.

"Speaking of sex." Tatum wanted to move on from the Blake conversation. "Can you please shed some light on this sugar baby situation?"

Nat rolled her eyes. "Let's get one thing straight. I *don't* have sex with him." She held up one hand. "I had to be three martinis deep to even *kiss* this man."

"You were like a bottle of Cuervo deep when you met JP on your first date, so that doesn't say much," Katelyn quipped.

"You know what I mean. He just gives me money and buys me clothes when I agree to go places with him. It started before Paris and I meant to end it but..."

Tatum interjected. "But what?"

"I don't know, the money is soooo good, you guys!"

Katelyn propped her head on the quilted pillow Nat had tossed off the couch. "Under different circumstances I'd say do whatever you want, but maybe it's not fair to JP."

"I mean, I guess it depends on how serious you want to be with him?" Tatum suggested. "Like if he's just a fling then who cares, but if you want a relationship, you either need to tell him or end it with Gramps."

"You already got the money," Katelyn said. "How much longer can this go on?"

Nat sighed. She knew her friends had a point. "I know. I

committed to an event with him for tonight and I can't back out of it. But after that, I'll end it."

"Wait, why can't you cancel tonight?" Tatum said. "Seems a little Christian Grey…"

Katelyn took a sip from her mug. "*Definitely* gray."

Nat grinned. "It's a tad complicated. I'm pretty much committed to the event when he pays me—it's part of our agreement. I can choose whenever I want to go, but if I accept the money, it kind of locks me in."

"So, I'm assuming you already accepted the money?" Tatum asked.

"All three thousand of it."

"*Three thousand dollars? Are you joking?*"

Katelyn jumped up from the floor and headed to the kitchen.

"First of all, that is so insane. I may have to find myself a dying rich man."

They heard a cupboard slamming open.

"Second of all, can I open these?"

Katelyn had already torn open a bag of organic dried mango and started munching.

"By all means," Nat said sarcastically. "Make yourself at home."

Katelyn came back to the living room, one hand stuck in the bag, the other scrolling her iPhone. "What? It's not like you can't afford more shitty fruit snacks."

■ ■ ■

Katelyn heard a loud clink as she threw her work bag on the small wooden table near her door.

What was that?

Hoping she hadn't smashed her phone, she ripped open the bag and rummaged through it. She found a wrapped package at the bottom. There was note scribbled in black marker:

This is for icing me out…but I love you anyway!

xoxo

Tatum

Katelyn opened the package to find a lukewarm bottle of iced tea. She laughed and took out her phone.

Katelyn: Got your final peace offering…
Tatum: I couldn't bring myself to buy a bottle of wine 🫠 still gagging at the sight of it

Katelyn looked at the time: 6:31 PM. She thought about the commitment she'd made to go out with Rachel, whose friends had a table at The Box that night. But as the time loomed nearer, the prospect of drinking watered-down cranberry vodkas and being hungover all Sunday seemed like the last thing she needed. She flung off her shoes, cracked open the bottle of iced tea, and grabbed last night's pad thai leftovers from the fridge.

Balancing everything, she flopped onto her unmade bed and wiggled under the covers. She opened her laptop and pressed Resume on "Bachelor In Paradise," then shoveled up some cold noodles with her chopsticks. Katelyn wasn't sure if it was making up with Tatum or the fact that spending the night alone seemed like a sign of healing, but she felt something she hadn't felt in weeks: a sense of internal peace.

21

NDA LEVEL-SHIT

Standing on the sidewalk in front of her apartment, Nat read the fifth rejection email on her phone and violently exhaled. Frustrated with her position at Marcheline, she'd started applying for jobs at different design firms and PR agencies in hopes of trying her hand in mainstream corporate America—only she'd forgotten how tedious and soul-sucking a job search could be. It was looking like the process would be long and daunting, and she wasn't really sure she could handle it.

"Hello Natalie," Marco said, startling her as he clicked open the back door of the shiny black Cadillac Escalade. She hadn't even noticed the car pull up.

"Bonsoir," Nat greeted him with a smile as she ducked into the backseat, clutching the side of her pink lace embroidered slip dress.

"And hello to you, Bill." She leaned in to kiss his withered cheek. This was the last time the two would be doing business together, and she was nervous to tell him. She figured being extra attentive the first half of the evening would lessen the blow—the only one he'd be getting that evening.

"You look terrific," he said, in the same low, raspy voice he always used when he was speaking to her. "And young, just like I asked. This is going to be a very special night." He put his arm around Nat and looked at her intensely.

"I'm excited to see what you have in store," she cooed, slightly uncomfortable. "Where are we going?" Bill had been vague about their evening plans all day, and Nat was getting impatient.

"I thought tonight would be a little different," he said, inching closer. "Instead of a private dinner, I'm taking you to a little party a few friends of mine are hosting."

"Oh fun," Nat lied, confused by the ambiguity in Bill's voice. "Where is this little *soirée?*"

Bill gently brushed Nat's cheek with the back of his dry hand. "Your skin is just glowing," he rasped. "You must *love* a facial." Then, oddly, he giggled.

Nat didn't even try to hide the disgust on her face. "Just good genetics!" she chirped, turning her head.

I hope for your sake that wasn't a sexual innuendo because I will jump out of this moving vehicle.

Bill sat stiff in his leather seat, visibly irritated by Nat's rejection.

"So," she said, sensing his annoyance, "where did you say this was?"

The car glided to a stop. "You're about to find out," he said, pressing the button to lower his tinted window.

A bald security guard stood outside the car, earpiece in place. "Hello Mr. Hayes," he nodded. "You're all set, enjoy your evening." He didn't so much as glance in Nat's direction.

"Thanks, Todd." Bill peeled two hundred-dollar bills from his Hermès money clip. "As always, your discretion is appreciated." He stuck his hand with the money out the window.

The bald man accepted the cash. "Thank you, Mr. Hayes." Bill smiled and rolled up the window.

Nat still didn't have the slightest idea where she was or what was going on, despite having caught a glimpse of a dimly lit parking lot behind the security guard. She looked over at Bill. "So, I can assume this isn't another poker game?" she asked, nervously patting the stray hairs on her slicked-back ponytail.

"Oh honey, this is a much more…*sensory* experience." His tongue lingered over his words as he leered at Nat.

Literally what now?

Nat tried her best to fake a smile as the back door of the car swung open. Marco stretched out his hand. "Miss Reardon." Nat took his hand and wiggled her way out of the car. Once she adjusted her dress, she looked around at the empty gray parking garage.

"Um," she said to Bill, who was making his way around the back of the car. "I won't lie to you; I *am* getting murderer vibes."

Bill laughed. "Oh, your imagination never ceases to amaze me." He took her hand. "Marco, figure a couple of hours," he said, leading the way towards an industrial door marked by a bold RESTRICTED AREA sign several feet away.

"Of course, enjoy," Marco replied, hopping back in the driver's seat, and shutting the car door. The Cadillac took off and Nat was left alone with Bill.

I swear to God, if I die at the hands of a sugar daddy in an abandoned parking garage I'm coming back as a ghost and haunting the shit out of him in his last days.

Bill pressed the button near the door and waited patiently for it to open after locking eyes with the small camera in the upper right-hand corner. The silence was heavy. "Natalie, relax; this is going to be fun," he murmured, clearly sensing her uneasiness. The door clicked open.

Nat peeked inside to a long, dark hallway. "After you," Bill gestured. She stepped into the hall and noted the dim LED lights on the ceiling that barely illuminated the cold, grey walls. She could feel Bill breathing behind her, his hand grazing her back as she took small steps toward the end of the passageway.

The farther they walked, the more Nat strained to hear any signs of life, but there was nothing but the sound of their steps. Finally, they arrived at a white door, barricaded with a thick brass bar. Next to the bar, a small pin pad was marked by a blinking red light. "Excuse me," Bill leaned over and punched in a series of numbers triggering three quick beeps.

"Go ahead," Bill said, in a soft, calm voice. The door was heavier than Nat had expected.

No wonder he wanted me to do this; he would've keeled over.

She cleared her throat and pushed the door open with force.

At first, Nat could only make out silhouettes of the crowd, but as she stepped inside the shapes took form. She could tell the guests were attractive, well-dressed individuals. She glanced around the dimly lit space and watched the attendees mingle as they sipped on brilliantly colored cocktails, clad in cartoonish ensembles.

Nat specifically took in the couple wearing matching Swarovski crystal-adorned harnesses, each holding a glowing balloon animal that served as a drink holder. Her eyes darted to the upholstered black wall outfitted with cuffs and four-point-restraints.

"Um. Where are we?"

Bill signaled the cocktail waiter who wore nothing but electric blue eyeliner and a fishnet jockstrap. He grabbed two gold-rimmed champagne flutes.

"I'm a part of a…secret club, let's say. And tonight, tonight is the crown jewel of all of our events."

She had never known Bill to be so mysterious and giddy. "And what *is* this secret club?"

Bill took another sip of his champagne and paused before answering. "An adult entertainment club."

Nat had to stop herself from spitting out her champagne. Choking on the fizzy drink, she blurted, "You mean like a *sex club?*"

Bill smiled and nodded. Nat was still processing this news when a tall, stunningly beautiful platinum blonde strutted over. Her six-foot frame was encased in a shiny latex bustier dress, perfectly pressing up her implants. The vertiginous Louboutin platforms she wore looked like a natural extension of her meticulously toned legs. She'd slicked her hair into a high, long ponytail that snaked down her back. A crystal birdcage mask covered the top half of her face, leaving her Angelina Jolie-esque lips in full view.

Okay, interesting career choice, lady. What happened in your life for you to end up here?

"Nice to see you again Bill," the sex robot purred, kissing him full on the mouth. Nat watched as the two exchanged an intimate hello.

What the hell?

"And who would this lovely creature be?" The woman gave Nat a full up-and-down appraisal. Nat was silent.

"This is Natalie," Bill replied, his voice filled with pride as he wrapped his arm around her narrow waist. Nat took a closer look at their hostess. Her plum-toned smokey eyeshadow was only partially visible through the birdcage, but it still enhanced her emerald, green eyes. Her full lips were stained a vampy purple. Enviably high cheekbones and a petite nose made her look more like a Russian supermodel than a swinger who hung around old pervs.

"Natalie, what a beautiful name." She leaned in and kissed Nat lingeringly on the lips, leaving a trail of her musky Floraïku perfume. "We're about to begin if you two want to take a seat. I saved the best view just for you, Bill."

She tapped him on the nose, flashed them a perfectly bleached smile. and glided back into the crowd as smoothly as she'd appeared.

"She's…something," said Nat. She polished off the last of her champagne in time to grab a fresh glass as the jock-strapped waiter passed by. She was hoping the booze would go to her head sooner rather than later.

"You haven't seen anything yet." Bill grabbed her hand and led her through the crowd. Nat was surprised to see people all ages— couples and singles alike. The guests wore fetish outfits that ranged from studded collars to schoolgirl jumpers. They made their way to a row of velvet seats at the front of the club.

Nat sat down and then started to sweat. They were nestled in plush crimson armchairs with a perfect view of a large glass panel that looked into a faintly-lit room. A large circular bed covered in what looked like a white bearskin throw sat front and center.

NO. FUCKING. WAY.

"Bill." Nat threw back the last of her second champagne. "I don't know if this is for me."

The room went black. Bill whispered in her ear, "Just relax, this is going to be groovy." The back of her neck felt prickly and hot.

A spotlight shined on the bed for a moment before the Russian-looking sex robot stepped into the frame wearing nothing but a sheer pink robe and her glittering veil, hair still tightly pulled back. Nat wasn't sure if she should laugh or scream as she watched the woman shimmy her way onto the bed, dropping the robe to reveal her nude body.

Nat's jaw dropped. "You're *joking*," she whispered, looking around the room to check the rest of the audience's reactions. She was met with disapproving stares, and a laser-focused Bill who couldn't keep his eyes off the show.

Unsure how else to process the situation, Nat nervously leaned back in the chair and examined the woman's statuesque curves as she lowered herself to the bed. Her legs looked even longer than they had moments before, the dramatic golden lighting perfectly emphasizing her slim waist and voluptuous fake breasts.

Okay, well she's definitely body goals.

The woman was crouched down on her hands and knees, cat-like, when the shadow of a hulking man appeared in the corner of the room. Apart from a bronze alligator mask, he was stark naked, all nine inches of him perfectly erect and unmistakably pierced. Nat heard a slight moan from a man sitting in front of her. She leaned over to see his rapidly moving hands as he jerked himself to the erotic display.

"Okay, I can't do this." Nat shot up from her seat and stormed towards the door.

"Natalie," she heard Bill hiss angrily as he got up to speed walk after her. She tried to feel her way towards the exit, disoriented by the lack of lighting and the two glasses of champagne she'd downed on an empty stomach.

"Natalie, *what are you doing?*" Bill pinched the back of her arm. "This is a performance and people are enjoying themselves."

"Yes, I can see that," she replied, not bothering to keep her voice down. "Look, Bill, I'm not doing this. Not just this bizarre sex show that you're using as some weird foreplay, but this whole arrangement."

She took a shuddering breath. "I think we need to stop seeing each other." Nat was grateful for the lack of lighting because she knew her words wouldn't have come out as boldly if she had been able to see Bill's face.

"This has run its course, and you should be spending your time and resources on somebody who enjoys being at…places like this." She could hear Bill's heavy breathing, but he didn't say anything.

After a long and uncomfortable pause, Bill said, "I thought you were different."

Nat sensed more disappointment than anger. "I know! I know you wanted this to work out and trust me, I did too. But it's just not for me anymore," she said, stretching out her arm to find his hand in the dark.

Please let me keep the money and clothes. Please let me keep the money and clothes.

Bill sighed. "You're a beautiful girl, Natalie, but you just don't have what it takes." The sex robot had started moaning during their conversation, and now she was at the point where her screaming orgasm was making their business breakup even more awkward.

"Take care," Nat said, patting Bill's shoulder. She was desperate to get out of there.

Without another word, Bill turned and went back to his seat. Nat watched him walk away, slumped over and sad. For a moment, she couldn't help but feel bad for him, for having used him the way she did. She debated calling after him until the sound of the man and woman grunting yanked her back to reality. She turned to the exit, just as she caught a glimpse of another male audience member with a pacifier around his neck squirting milk from a baby bottle into his mouth.

This place is a fucking zoo.

She forgot about her temporary pity towards Bill.

Not what you'd expect from the 1%...

Nat felt around, finally recognizing the shape of a brass knob. She pushed the door open with all of her body weight and barreled down the dark hallway. She flung open the industrial entrance and stepped into the empty parking garage. Already, she could hear the sounds of Manhattan and she breathed a long sigh of relief.

She looked around for an exit, walking rapidly to a well-lit staircase, then opened her Celine clutch and found her phone. She glanced down at the blue screen, confused to see two missed calls from JP. She trotted down the last of the stairs, dialing his number as she stepped onto the busy NYC sidewalk. She stood by the garage entrance and put the phone to her ear only to hear his voicemail. She tried again; the call again went straight to voicemail.

Baffled, she tucked the phone back in her clutch and looked up at the bright, pulsing lights of the city. For a fleeting moment, she forgot all about the sex club and JP. Nat's stomach growled aggressively, reminding her she hadn't eaten all day in anticipation of a decadent dinner out. Eying a street cart on the next corner, she bolted across the street and walked right up to the vendor.

"Hi there, can I get a hotdog with yellow mustard and relish and a large Coke please?" The man nodded and started preparing her order. Nat took out her phone to try JP again.

"That'll be six-fifty," the man said, handing Nat a paper boat with her food.

She smiled and wedged her phone under her arm to pay. "Thank you," she said, handing the man a ten. "Keep the change."

I could use some good karma.

Juggling her food and the iPhone, Nat scurried to the sidewalk by the cart and took a seat on the curb. She couldn't care less that the pavement was dirtying her Balenciaga lace dress. In that moment, free from sex-crazed Bill, liberated from that odious room, Nat couldn't be happier to be indulging in cheap street food by a rancid sewer, observing fellow New Yorkers going about their Saturday night.

■ ■ ■

Where the hell are my keys?

Nat fumbled for her fluffy keychain as she strode down the hall to her apartment door. After a longer than anticipated Uber drive home and one too many catcalls from randoms on her way up the block, Nat couldn't wait to make herself a chai latte and enjoy the last of her Saturday night in the safety and security of her bedroom.

"Where have you been?" Nat jumped when she heard a man's voice. She looked up from her bag and saw a defeated JP, slouched over on the floor outside her door, a wilted bodega bouquet next to him.

"What are you doing here?" she asked, walking towards him.

"Nat, I've been calling you all night," he said, standing. Nat could tell he was nervous.

"I tried calling you back, but it went straight to voicemail," she said. "How long have you been here?"

JP bent and gently kissed her lips. "My phone died—so maybe an hour?" He slid his hands around the back of her neck. "Listen. I came here because I want to talk to you. I know we haven't been completely honest with each other."

Oh My God, he knows about Bill.

"What do you mean?" She racked her brain, trying to think how she would explain herself. "Look JP, I planned on telling you…"

"Nat, please let me say this." He pressed his index finger to her lips. "I like you."

Alright, where is this going?

"And I don't want to just keep casually dating. I don't want to be in some limbo thing. I want to date you—like boyfriend-girlfriend date you," he stared into her eyes. "I know I should have told you sooner, especially because I've known how I felt about you since before you went to Paris. I can't stop thinking about you. I wake up thinking about you. I go to sleep thinking about you. Every time your name comes up on my phone, I get this dumb smile on my face. I want to make you mine and prove to you that I can make your life incredible."

Nat smiled and answered without a hint of hesitation, surprising herself with the directness of her answer. "JP, I'm falling in love with you. I have been for a while."

In that moment she realized she was ready for intimacy and commitment, something she was admitting to herself as much as to JP.

"And, I'm sorry. I know I've been all over the place these last few weeks, but if there's one thing I feel sure about, it's you."

She leaned in and pressed her mouth to his, feeling happier than ever that Bill was officially in the past, and that her future was right in front of her. She dropped her clutch on the carpeted hallway as JP passionately pressed her up against the wall.

"So, boyfriend, huh," she said between kisses.

"Get used to it," he smiled as he hoisted her up. "Oh, and now you definitely have to meet my mom."

And I thought the dirty-water dog was going to be the highlight of my night.

22

THE HEIRLOOM

"So, I thought for sure he knew about Bill, but then he said he wanted to be official," Nat reported, propping her phone against a glass vase on the coffee table. She reached for the cleaning spray and furiously misted the table.

"I'm so happy for you," Tatum said, her face distorted on the FaceTime screen she was holding too close. "I know you've been wanting this for a long time, so I'm really glad you found a good guy, Nat."

"And it doesn't hurt that he's going to be a *doctor*," Katelyn chimed in from her screen, "even though I'm swearing off them for good."

"A dentist—but thanks you guys, that means a lot." Nat wiped at the coffee table, knowing Julia could walk into their dirty apartment at any moment. "Oh Katelyn!" she exclaimed. "I forgot to tell you. You'll never guess who I saw at Starbucks the other day, and he was asking about you."

"Who?" Katelyn replied. She was propped on her bed with a highlighter in hand, and she didn't look up from her textbook.

"Deane Friar," Nat said enthusiastically. "You know, from high school? He was *so into you* back in the day and now that you're a single lady...I think you should give him a shot!"

"Oh my God, *yes*," Tatum agreed, the sounds of the City radiating from her background. "He used to ask you out all the time, Kate! He's so cute too." She was walking down a busy Manhattan street as she talked. She'd given up trying to show her face on her screen, instead subjecting the girls to a view of the scaffolding over her head.

"You guys." Katelyn finally looked up at her screen. "Deane Friar used to eat flowers at recess in middle school. I don't think I can get past that. Besides, didn't he date that gorgeous blonde two grades below us? I doubt he's interested." She looked back down at the pile of books in front of her.

"Okay, I didn't know about the flower thing and while that *is* disturbing, you're a hot tamale and why *wouldn't* he be interested?" Tatum's screen showed busy traffic as she waited to cross an intersection.

"Enough about Deane Friar." Katelyn stuck a pencil in the floppy bun on the top of her head. "Tatum, what's the deal with you and Blake? Have things been good?"

Katelyn and Nat were hoping to read Tatum's face, but she was now treating them to the image of a pigeon eating a hamburger wrapper.

"Um..." Tatum hedged. "I mean, we talked everything through, and while it sucked to break up, we think we both learned a lot. I feel a lot more independent this time around, and I know it may not look like that because he cheated, but I decided for myself that I just want him in my life, not *need* him necessarily."

Nat stepped back into frame with a vacuum in hand. "I'm really proud of you! What a mature response."

"As long as you're happy," Katelyn conceded.

"Well thank you, guys." Tatum was walking down the stairs to the subway. "I'm about to lose you—I'm getting on the subway now; we'll chat later!"

Katelyn reached toward her phone. "I better get back to studying anyway." She blew the camera a kiss.

"And I have to finish cleaning before Julia shows up!" Nat held her nose. "I need a clean apartment before she starts firing up the kimchi again. *Ciao!*"

■ ■ ■

"Hey babe!" Tatum called as she locked the heavy apartment door behind her. It had been nearly a month since she and Blake had gotten back together, and while their relationship had changed since the breakup, she couldn't help but enjoy their easy familiarity.

While Tatum had wanted to take things slow, Blake ended up moving in only two weeks after her 25th birthday. "Blake?" she asked again, tossing her keys on the counter and dropping her heavy tote on the floor.

"In here," Blake yelled from the other end of the apartment.

"I was thinking we could do sushi for dinner," she shouted, slipping off her leather loafers, "and sooner rather than later because I'm starving." She waited for Blake to answer but didn't hear a thing. "Helloooo, are you there?!" She walked down the hall and to her bedroom. "I've been talking to yo—"

Tatum went silent as she stood in the doorway. She looked around, taking in the candlelit room with red rose petals strewn across the floor. Candles were arranged on the floor in the shape of a semi-circle, surrounding a very nervous, clean-cut Blake. He was wearing the navy-blue suit he'd rented for a friend's wedding a few weeks before.

"Hi honey." He stood with his hands clasped in front of him, his usual messy hair meticulously gelled back. Tatum was taken aback by the whole scene.

"Blake, what are you doing?"

He flashed his perfect smile at her. "Come here," he said, holding out his hands.

Tatum walked closer, through the rose petals until her hands were interlocked with his. "You and I have been through so much together and I need you to know how much I love and appreciate you," he said, his big green eyes staring into hers. Tatum could feel her heart beating fast. "I've known you were the one since I saw you."

He took a breath. Tatum could tell he was trying to calm his nerves. "And it took me losing you to realize that I will do whatever it takes to make you happy for the rest of our lives." Blake gently released Tatum's hands and went down on one knee, taking a small black box from the pocket of his dress pants.

"Oh my God Blake," Tatum's voice cracked as her eyes filled with tears. She moved her hands over her mouth as Blake opened the box to reveal a glimmering solitaire ring.

"Tatum Rose Kelley," he said, raising the ring. "Will you marry me?"

Tatum's mind was flooded with more emotions than she'd known were humanly possible.

Fuck. I love him but he cheated on me. And I asked him to take it slow. But he's the one, right? Lola. Fuck. What will everyone think? My parents love him. Life with him is all I've ever wanted…right?

She pushed all her doubts aside. "Yes! Yes, of course, I will!" Tatum screamed. Blake stood and hoisted her small body as she wrapped her legs around his waist, tears streaming down her face.

"Can't forget this," he said, placing her back on her feet and opening the box again.

Tatum wiped the tears from her eyes as she took in the sparkling two-carat, emerald cut diamond in an elegant gold setting.

"This is stunning." She watched Blake take the ring out of its slot and slide it onto her perfectly manicured finger.

"Do you like it? It was my grandmother's. She said she knew as soon as she met you that you'd be the one to wear it."

Tatum stared down at the glittering rock on her hand. She threw her arms around Blake, nervously twirling the diamond on her left ring finger with her thumb.

"I can't wait to marry you, future Mrs. Spencer," he whispered in her ear.

"I have to call my mom," Tatum said, staring down at her hand.

"Actually, you don't. Both of our parents are waiting for us at Nobu. We're going to head over as soon as you get dressed."

"How did you know I wanted sushi tonight?" Tatum asked as she leaned in to kiss him.

"You're going to be my wife; it's my job to know."

Tatum tried to smile enthusiastically, unable to say anything else.

■ ■ ■

"Let me see that!" Nat grabbed Tatum's outstretched hand to get a closer look at the delicate diamond on her dainty ring finger. "I cannot *believe* you're getting married!!" she shrieked. "AND that I get to be a bridesmaid!" She rotated Tatum's finger to get a full visual of her friend's new heirloom.

"It's beautiful," Katelyn confirmed, looking over Nat's shoulder. She glanced at the ring and leaned back in her chair. "I just…" Katelyn paused. "Never mind," she said, taking a sip of the generous mimosa she'd poured from the carafe in the center of the table.

"What?" Tatum asked, gently pulling her hand from Nat's grip.

Katelyn set her drink down. "You know that I'm happy for you, and after everything that's happened, you know that's all I want is for you to be happy."

"Okaaay," Tatum replied cautiously.

"But don't you think it's a little soon? I mean you guys *just* got back together," Katelyn sighed as she looked down at the table, "I don't want you to feel like you're rushing into anything. Plus, after the whole Lola thing, I thought…."

"Look," Tatum said cutting off her friend as she leaned over the table towards Katelyn. "I know you just want what's best for me. I've wanted to marry Blake since I was a junior in college. Yes, he made mistakes. I've thought about that and at the end of the day, that's in the past. I know he's the one." Tatum reached over and took Katelyn's hand.

"Then that's all the confirmation I needed," Katelyn said. "Now let me see that ROCK!" Tatum smiled and exaggeratedly flipped her hair as she stretched out her hand again.

"I would not be able to keep my eyes off my hand if I were you," Nat said, flagging down the nearest waiter.

"I can't! Every time I look down, I'm in shock," Tate said with a dry laugh.

"Have you guys started talking about the wedding?" Nat

asked. "Wedding...so weird to say," she giggled, as the waiter approached the table. "Hi there. I know we just ordered mimosas, but our friend here just got engaged so we'll need your largest bottle of champagne."

"Well, congratulations! He sure is a lucky man," the waiter said. "And let me see that *stone!*" He reached for Tatum's hand. She timidly stuck out her arm as the waiter leaned in close. "Oh my God... and it looks like you're one lucky girl. I'll be right back with your bottle of bubbly!" Tatum gazed down at her hand once more. Her stomach tingled every time she looked at the ring.

"Soooo...the wedding?" Katelyn demanded, tapping the table impatiently.

Tatum sipped her mimosa. "We're leaning towards South Carolina."

"Aww, doesn't Blake have family down there?" Nat chimed in.

"Yeah, his mom is from there. Connecticut is great, but my parents are totally on board with a southern wedding. It's so beautiful and his grandma still lives there and she's not in the best shape to travel up here or anything."

"Do you guys have a timeline?" Nat picked at the mini scone on her plate.

"Probably not for a little while," Tatum said. "We're not there financially, and plus we still have to work some things out."

"Whenever the day comes, I'm sure it will be beautiful," Nat replied with her mouth full.

"So, I have over a year to find a plus one—let's start praying now, shall we?" Katelyn raised her phone high above the table to snap a pic of the pre-brunch setup, accented by Tatum's glamorous left hand.

"Hey, if all else fails, dare I propose Deane Friar?" Nat sipped at the straw of her sparkling water.

"As long as he doesn't eat my centerpieces!" Tatum threw a mini scone in her mouth. Katelyn and Nat were laughing as the waiter reappeared with a chilled bottle of off-brand champagne. He put a bucket of ice on the girls' table and presented the label.

"It's our best bottle," he said, unscrewing the metal ring. "Here's to a long, happy, and saaaaaaatisfying marriage!" He popped the seal, launching the cork at the ceiling. The girls clapped.

"One penis for the rest of your life," Katelyn shrugged, swigging the last of her mimosa before putting her empty glass in front of the waiter.

Tatum laughed nervously and raised her glass.

For now.

■ ■ ■

"I was thinking for the engagement party we could do that vineyard by my parents, since the wedding's going to be in Charleston," Tatum said, not looking at Blake as she flipped through *Martha Stewart Weddings* on her couch.

"Tate," Blake said, staring at the Yankees game on the TV from the other end of the loveseat. Tatum glanced up from her magazine. "I know you're really excited about this, and I am too, but I thought we agreed we weren't getting married for a bit. Do we really need to be thinking about engagement parties and vineyards and all that right now?"

Tatum stared at him as she flipped the magazine shut, tossing it on the coffee table. "I think we should be prepared so when the time comes, we know what we want." She couldn't help but felt a tinge of embarrassment.

"And we will, but not *years* in advance," he said. "I mean who knows, maybe in three years or so we'll want to just go down to city hall." His voice trailed off as he adjusted his backwards baseball hat and leaned back with the remote.

"*Three years?*" Tate sat up. "I thought we said eighteen months or two years max."

"Listen, babe, all I'm saying is that I'm not in a rush. I don't think we should be planning a wedding when we don't even know when we'll be *ready* to get married." He glanced at her briefly before returning his attention to the TV screen.

"Then why did you propose?!" Tatum blinked back tears as she jumped up from the couch and walked towards the bathroom.

"I knew you were going to do this," Blake sighed, not getting up. "I proposed to you because I love you and I want to marry you...*eventually*. But obviously, we aren't ready right *now*."

Tatum slammed the bathroom door and slumped down behind it, staring at the gorgeous diamond ring on her hand. "Tatum," she heard Blake coax from the other side of the door. "Don't get all upset. We're going to get married, just not soon."

"I know," she snapped, wiping the snot from her nose. "You made that *perfectly* clear." She waited for his next response but heard only footsteps walking away.

"Take a hot shower and I'll order some dinner," Blake said nonchalantly from the direction of the kitchen.

Tatum thought about how volatile their relationship had become since they broke up. While she loved the idea of an intimate southern wedding with her gorgeous fiancée, she hadn't really considered what married life would be like with Blake. She stood and looked in the mirror, her mascara smudged under her eyes.

I can't do this…can I?

She closed her eyes as the tears continued to stream down her face, thinking first about the night she met Blake, then about the video.

The video! What am I doing?!

Her tears turned to rage as she flung open the bathroom door and walked out to find an indifferent Blake standing in the kitchen scrolling on his phone.

"I'm not doing this." Tatum wiped away the remnants of her tears with the back of her hand, the two-carat diamond brushing her face.

"Baby, what are you talking about? C'mon let's go watch TV."

"No!" Tatum locked eyes with Blake, her fury mounting with every second. "I don't know *what* I was thinking." She scanned him up and down. "You cheated on me with that—," she trailed off, "how could we ever be together?" She strode out of the kitchen and back to their bedroom, Blake trotting behind. She pulled out a duffle bag from the closet and tossed it onto the bed, then started rummaging through her drawers.

"Tate, we talked about this, and I said I'm sorry. You can't hold it over my head forever. Plus, maybe, if you had paid a little bit more attention to me instead of work all the time, I wouldn't have felt the need to look somewhere else for it."

Tatum could feel her face flush with frustration. "*Excuse* me?" She turned slowly. "YOU are blaming ME for the fact that you cheated? Like your fetish of getting peed on in a dingy hotel is something *I'm* responsible for? I've hardly been able to look at you these past few weeks without thinking of some redhead crouching over you. Every time I'm in the bathroom I wonder if you're hanging around outside getting a boner listening to me pee."

"Tatum."

"I'm not done." She feverishly moved her hands to her hips. "Of *course*, you're not ready to get married, Blake—you're a child. You can't think about anyone but yourself. You live in this apartment that you don't pay a dime for. The only real date we've been on in the past five years was our engagement dinner that *my* parents paid for. You couldn't even buy me a ring of my own, you just *handed* me one that was given to you!"

She puffed out her chest, feeling more in control than she ever had in her life.

Blake stuck his lower lip out, making him look more toddler-like than ever. "You know what, you're right. We can't get married. How could I have such a *bitch* of a wife!"

"Well, I could never have such a freeloading *loser* as a husband, whose only redeeming quality is his hot cousin—who I already hooked up with!"

Blake swallowed hard as he glared at Tatum. "What did you just say?"

"Yeah, let's just say Lola and I really *did* hit it off after all. Turns out one night with her was more life-changing than the five years I wasted with you." Tatum could see Blake had nothing to say, his mouth gaped open and his face had gone stark white. "I don't know why I'm packing a bag. I pay the rent here, so *you* actually need to leave."

"I just—"

"Leave, please." Tatum cut him off abruptly. "And don't forget *this.*" She slid the ring off her finger and put it on the dresser as she walked out the door. She tried not to make eye contact with Blake as she brushed past him and strode down the hallway. "I need some fresh air. When I get back, I expect you to be gone."

"Tatum," Blake's voice cracked.

"Blake. It's *over.*" She slid on her Keds and slammed the front door behind her.

23

HOME SWEET CHICAGO

Katelyn stepped off the subway and breathed in the fall morning air she'd waited for all summer long. She buttoned her thick beige wool cardigan over her scrubs and began the short walk to her new favorite coffee shop, conveniently close to Lennox Hill Hospital.

She'd always loved NYC in the morning. Half the people were ending their night while the other half were starting their day. She felt her most rejuvenated drinking a to-go coffee as the sun rose over the gleaming metal skyline. Her budget allowed her a coffee treat only twice a week as opposed to the burnt pot of Folger's she made for herself most mornings. And since today was a gourmet coffee day, she knew it had to be a good one.

Katelyn stepped inside the new sustainable coffee shop. The eco-atmosphere of the small space was elevated by a greenery wall that looked more like an art installation; the same wall that had made an appearance in Timothée Chalamet's Instagram only a week before. Katelyn stood in the back of the line behind the mess of people restlessly awaiting their morning lifeline. She read the menu on the magnetic letter board behind the register and snapped her AirPod case closed, tossing it into her shoulder tote.

"Can I please get a medium latte with oat milk and two pumps of pumpkin spice?" She reached into her bag to fish for her wallet. "Oh, and an almond croissant, thanks." She pointed to the fluffy, freshly baked pastries in the glass window. The woman at the register tapped her screen and yelled the order to the barista behind her.

"Katelyn Coppola?"

Katelyn looked back over her shoulder. "It *is* Katelyn, right?" asked a blonde man standing behind her.

"Um, yes?" Katelyn responded, confused.

Did I drop my hospital ID badge?

"Oh, I'm sorry. This is probably so weird for you."

The man inched closer to Katelyn, who was still searching for her wallet.

"Gavin Sheppard. We went to middle school together—I know your brother."

"Excuse me, ma'am?" The woman behind the counter interrupted their stare-off. "That'll be thirteen sixty-two and there's a *line.*"

Alright lady I'm trying and there's a hot guy talking to me so give me a break.

"Oh, right, my bad," Katelyn propped her bag on one knee and began furiously rummaging.

"Let me get this," he said, leaning over Katelyn and giving his card to the cashier. "And add a cold brew to that order as well."

"No, really. That's nice of you but I know it's in here—"

"I insist."

"Thank you, that's really sweet." Katelyn tried to hide her flushed cheeks as she hitched her bag strap to her shoulder. "So, you said you know Carter?"

"Yeah, we played town lacrosse together. Our parents are pretty good friends, too." Katelyn felt bad because she could tell he was slightly embarrassed that she had no idea who he was. She nodded her head just as it came to her.

SCRAWNY GAVIN SHEPPARD?!

"Oh my God, Gavin, yes. Of *course*, I remember you. Wow, you look so different," Katelyn said, stunned by his new looks. This handsome, charming man in a perfectly fitted suit was a far cry from the skinny, pimply boy she remembered from childhood. "You look *great,*" she blurted out as they shuffled to the pickup counter.

He laughed. "Thank you. Yeah, well things could only improve from the last time you saw me."

Katelyn giggled.

"I actually just moved to the City and believe it or not, I don't know that many people."

Another pissed-off barista reached over with two cups of coffee, then dumped the croissant bag on the counter. Gavin took them both and handed Katelyn her latte.

"I'd love any recommendations you have—or anything like that," he said.

Katelyn took the latte and sipped, staring up at Gavin's mischievous brown eyes.

"Yeah, definitely," she replied, not breaking eye contact. "I actually work around the block so if you're not pressed for time I can give you a three-minute intro to the City?"

"Yeah, that'd be perfect." Gavin looked relieved. "I don't have to be in court for another hour or so."

An attorney, nice.

"So, what brought you to the City?" Katelyn asked, pushing the door open and stepping onto the sidewalk.

"Well," he paused to take a sip of his iced coffee. "I was up in Boston for about five years after I graduated college to go to law school. I temped up there for a big firm for a bit. It wasn't until a few months back when I got out of a pretty serious relationship, I thought—why not?"

His long legs easily matched with Katelyn's stride. "I've always wanted to work in the City, so here we are."

"Well, this City's definitely not for the faint of heart," she joked. "But I think you'll find it'll be a welcome change."

"I think it will be."

Katelyn felt him staring at her profile. She stopped outside of the hospital. "This is me."

"Should I be calling you Dr. Coppola?"

"Just PA student Coppola for now."

"It was really good to see you. I was hoping this block would be a little longer."

Katelyn blushed again.

"Why don't I get your number?" he asked. "And maybe you can give me a better rundown of the City over dinner?" He reached into his suit pocket and pulled out his phone. Katelyn smiled when she caught a glimpse of the picture of him and his parents on the screen.

"To be honest," she said, staring at the phone in his hand, "I'm not really dating right now." It was the first time Katelyn had ever rejected a guy. "It's nothing personal. Trust me you seem great; I'm just really trying to focus on school these days."

"Two breakups in one year!" he joked, his hand still clutching his phone, "I completely understand. Tell you what, my office is only a few blocks up so how about if you ever need a lunch break buddy, you let me know. As friends."

"Now *that* sounds perfect."

■ ■ ■

Katelyn made her way through the hospital doors, greeted immediately by a bubbly Rachel, who grabbed her forearm. *"Tell me* you heard the med school drama."

"Let me guess, someone's dad got them into the program and now they have to update the nepotism policy…again," Katelyn's voice trailed off as she took in the swarms of students giddily buzzing around.

"Apparently one of the students was caught sending *porn* around with his student email! Dr. Danver received some perverted link to a fetish site that started playing in front of a patient." Rachel's eyes widened as she went on. "They launched an investigation and found he had like so many porn sites on his phone and was sending all of these fucked-up porn videos to other students AND teachers from his email, can you believe it?!"

"Wow. Now what kind of sick person would do that?"

"Attention please," Dr. Danver's voice cut through the chatter. "I'm sure some of you have heard by now that we had an incident with one of your peers regarding inappropriate content. While we are not going to disclose the details of the investigation, said student has been suspended from our program temporarily. I will also take this time to re-iterate that we take our morality clause very seriously. If we find out that any other student is in violation, there will be serious repercussions."

Katelyn smiled as she looked down, Peter's face flashing in her mind for just a second.

You were right, this isn't my first rodeo, asshole.

■ ■ ■

Nat glanced at her phone and saw an unread message from JP:

`Good luck on your first day babe` 🔥💀

She smiled and sent back a kissy-face emoji, tossing her near-empty coffee in the metal trash can in front of her new office building. She took a moment to watch the swarms of young people hopping up the stairs with their laptop cases and headphones, their casual tees and sneakers already a far cry from her glamorous colleagues at Marcheline.

After examining her reflection in the mirrored building, Nat approached the entrance, still unrecognizable with her shiny, dark brown hair. She was proud of the "first day" outfit she'd spent so much time picking out the night before—a chunky knit sweater paired with dark wash jeans, and in typical Nat fashion, sky-high knee boots. Stepping into the grand lobby staged with elaborate coffee stations and modern seating, she felt the buzz from the young professionals around her and a new sense of confidence filled her, one that she'd forgotten about since working at Marcheline.

"Hi, I'm Natalie Reardon," she said to the thirty-something woman holding a tablet in the doorway of the conference room.

"Got it!" the woman chirped. "Welcome to Upcycle. Help yourself to a canvas tote and a green juice on your way in!"

She directed Nat to a large round table inside. Nat smiled and stepped into the state-of-the-art conference room and took a seat in one of the ergonomic office chairs in front of a neon sign that read, "ECO-FRIENDLY FASHION IS NOT A TREND. IT'S THE FUTURE." She looked out the window at the breathtaking view of a metallic NYC horizon against the crystal blue sky, then at the two other people sitting across from her.

"Hey, I'm Nat," she said, smiling in their direction. One of them, a girl with curly black hair and a perfect cat eye, put her green juice down and smiled.

"Jameson," she said. "Your first day?"

"Yes! They hired me last week." Nat twisted the gold bangle on her wrist. "I needed a change of pace."

"Trust me, I get it. I love your outfit," Jameson replied. "This place is great. You're absolutely going to love working with the designers; they're so talented."

"I'm Luca." The boy sitting on the other side of the table gave an awkward wave. Nat noticed he looked older. "I worked on Wall Street for years. I guess I needed a change of pace, too," he said.

"That would explain the Tom Ford suit," Nat smiled. Luca let out a hearty laugh.

"Welcome everyone!"

The room fell silent as the woman who'd been manning the door with her tablet made her way to the front of the room, four more new faces shuffling to their seats in her wake. "My name's

Lori, and I'm so excited to welcome Luca and Natalie to the Upcycle team!" she announced in an over-enthused voice.

"I know you probably haven't gotten a chance to chat with each other and seeing as community is one of our brand pillars, I thought we could make our new additions feel welcome with some team ice breakers!"

Icebreakers?

Nat watched Lori take a sip from a stainless-steel coffee mug that read #environmentalism.

Kill me now.

Lori broke into a wide grin. "I'm kidding you guys, this isn't the '90s, we're not doing icebreakers." The room filled with laughter. "You'll have plenty of time to get to know each other at the team wellness session later. For now, we have to talk through the Brooklyn space for the show the Adams Brothers are putting on for the debut of their couture collection. Everything's made from recycled Nespresso pods!"

Nat breathed in excitedly and took her slender laptop out of her bag.

Finally.

■ ■ ■

Tatum taped the last of her moving boxes shut and flopped down on the bare floor. It had been six weeks since she called off her engagement to Blake. After the initial shock wore off, she knew she needed a change. After talking herself out of getting bangs and contemplating an overpriced gym membership, Tatum finally settled on the dramatic shift she felt she really needed: moving.

A promotion to Everett's Chicago office had come up as Tatum's lease was ending, which made her decision even more satisfying. She took the job and found a perfect one-bedroom in Gold Coast when she'd flown out with her mom only a month before. In 24 hours Tatum would be on the road to Illinois, the only relics of her NYC life packed in a U-Haul.

Now, staring at the blank walls in the empty room once filled with images of her life with Blake, Tatum felt relieved. She stretched out her slender legs and took her phone from the strap of her plunging sports bra. She clicked it open and tapped on the app store, perusing the suggested dating apps.

Just see what's out there! It's time.

She clicked on the first one and hit Download. A welcome screen appeared prompting her to create an account, a video of a happy couple playing Frisbee in the background. She typed in her name and her email, which quickly prompted the next screen:

"What are your dating preferences: Male, Female, or Both?"

She stared down at her phone, nervously biting her bottom lip.

Screw it.

She clicked "Both."

A message from Just Us Girls appeared at the top of her screen:

Katelyn: I'm coming straight from work, so forgive me Tatum if your last visual of me is fugly.

Tatum smiled.

Nat: I'm super casual today too just a tee-shirt and jeans

Katelyn: But Natalie, I want you to look young!
Nat: Venmo me a couple of g's and I'll see what I
    can do
Tatum: Leaving now!

Tatum giggled as she shut off her phone, realizing if she didn't start making her way downtown, she'd be late for her farewell "pies and pints" dinner. Katelyn had come up with the name, of course. She'd arranged for the three girls to meet at a hole-in-the-wall pizza joint so Tatum could get "one final New York slice" before she left. She stood up from the floor and exhaled as she looked around the apartment one more time.

"Good riddance."

■ ■ ■

"Let's get one of each. Fuck it. This is a celebration," Katelyn slammed the paper menu down and raised the murky glass of Guinness to her lips.

"*Désolée*, you guys!" Nat's cheery voice floated towards the standing table where Tate and Katelyn were already situated. The sound of pickup orders and kitchen commands nearly masked her entrance.

"Hey Greta Thunberg, you're late," Katelyn smiled as she watched Nat prop her vegan leather tote on the leg of the table.

"Good things come to people who wait!" Nat grinned. "And YOU." She threw her arms around Tatum. "Please tell me that you changed your mind and decided to stay in the concrete jungle forever with me."

"You'll just have to come and visit me in Chi-town," Tatum retorted. "It'll be like the Sisterhood of the Traveling Pants!"

"So long as there's a sexual Grecian specimen to sweep me off my feet!" Katelyn took another swig of her dark beer. Nat unfolded herself from Tatum and pushed her hair behind her neck with one hand, stealing Katelyn's beer with the other.

"I'd like to propose a toast," she announced, pouring a splash of Katelyn's drink into one of the ridged water cups stacked near the napkin holder.

"Hey, you don't even drink beer!"

"It's a special occasion. Now," Nat raised her glass, "this will probably be the first of many toasts this evening—" The two other girls raised their glass pints. "But…"

"Yo, you gotta step over here. We got people pickin' up and I'm trying to get these out the door, so I don't block the servers," the balding gruff man from behind the counter yelled at their table.

"Well, maybe if you took our order instead of acting like the Gordon Ramsay of dollar slices, we'd be out of here by now," Katelyn said. "Anyway," she straightened and raised her glass even higher, "go on."

"I'm going to miss that New York hospitality," Tatum giggled.

"Anyway—as I was saying. We've had *quite* the summer ladies, and I feel so blessed to have you both in my life. I don't know what I would do without you." Nat could feel her eyes tearing up as she stared across the minuscule table at Katelyn and Tatum.

"You'd probably still be sucking off senior citizens," Katelyn joked.

"AND," Nat continued, shooting a playful look at Katelyn, "As much as it pains me that the three of us will no longer be in the same city, Tatum, I'm so proud of you, and I've already booked my ticket to visit for early December."

"I can't wait," Tatum beamed. "Here's to the nights we'll never remember, with the friends we'll never forget!"

"I love you, but that was so cringe," Katelyn laughed.

"I saw it on the Internet. It sounded better in my head."

"To best friends," Nat corrected.

"To best friends!" The girls clinked their glasses in unison.

Printed in the USA
CPSIA information can be obtained
at www.ICGtesting.com
LVHW040254271123
765002LV00036B/596

9 798218 299279